Other novels

Silent Violence
Nails
Bottle
Deutschisch
Ausländer
More

Short story collections

...and the man who loved cats

Novellas

Josephine's kiln

About the author

David M. Samson, born in Wallasey (near Liverpool), lives
with his wife and two daughters in Germany.

...and two men on a mountain

First published in 2023 by David M. Samson

ISBN 978-0-9556796-9-8

British Library Cataloguing in Publication Data.
A catalogue record for this book is available from the British Library.

Cover design by David M. Samson (original photograph with thanks to www.hippopx.com).

www.davidmsamson.com

I have paved the way – removing stones and garbage and shards – to the passages you are about to travel. Essentially we take similar journeys and I hope you enjoy taking them as much as I did creating them.

D.M. Samson
(October 2023)

...and two men on a mountain

The occupant of room twelve

"You're dead," was the first thing the occupant of room twelve said to me when I went in to give him his meds that very first time.

"Charming, I'm sure," I muttered to myself. Instead I said loud and clear: "Sorry?"

You have to talk loud and clear to them all, otherwise you'll find yourself repeating it. Yes, one occasionally hears replies of: "I'm not deaf." But the odds are weighted against such protests.

I had unlocked the small medicine cabinet just inside his door and was looking at the chart upon which we documented his medication. He was sitting in a stiff wing-backed chair positioned with its back to the window and looking at me.

"You're dead," he repeated.

I chose not to say: "I'm more alive than you are, you old fool." I concentrated on getting his meds right. Make a mistake with them and you'd be out of a job. Of course, the recipient of the wrong medication could be worse off.

Gregory Mason was on tablets to stop him having another stroke. He received a concoction of pills three times a day.

I tipped the plastic cup containing the pills into his

hand. I thought the rigmarole of putting the pills in a cup and then tipping them out was pointless, but that was one of the rules. I also had to watch the act of swallowing, stopping short of asking them to poke out and lift their tongue.

He wasn't a bad looking gent for his age – one of the few male residents here. There was a distinguished air about him, as if he was waiting for someone to bring in the cigars and brandy. Fat chance here. And anyway, his medication prohibited alcohol.

He wore a gold ring on the little finger of his left hand. At one time there may have been something etched on the face of it, lettering or an insignia or the like, but it was long gone and such wear hinted at heirloom, rather than a defacing within a single generation. On closer inspection individual anomalies contradicted this overall impression. Hair that had thickened with time to resemble bristles sprouted from the back of his fingers. A tangle of wire inhabited his nostrils like poorly-made birds' nests. His ears too could do with some earnest plucking. Incongruously his eyebrows were thick and dark, reminding one of a character from the Muppet show, for his hair was white, matching his silver sideburns.

"What's with the toff in room twelve," I asked Wendy when she came into the staff room during my morning break.

Although I'd worked in the home for more than five months, I had until now been upstairs and was just getting to know the residents and staff there, when the boss shifted me downstairs. So I had to start all over again getting acquainted with everyone.

"Mr. Mason?"

"Yeah him. He said I was dead."

"Take no notice, Mo." I liked that she called me Mo. I hated the name Morag and insisted everyone called me Mo. Only the boss called me Morag. Stupid bitch. But then she called everyone by their full first names. I got the impression this was a concession on her part and she would have preferred surnames only. Yeah, snooty.

"Gregory's harmless," Wendy continued. "He comes and goes. The rest are off their heads."

"We are too," I said, "doing this for a job."

I guess I didn't take to Mason from the start. Not merely because of his statement, but because he was typical of this place. On the one hand, it was good to work in a high-end home. The staff was friendly and helpful, overly kind and patient. But this was as much a curse as a virtue. I was expected to be the same. You had to learn to bottle up your frustration. And some days it was enough to make you scream.

You see, most of the staff were working class aspiring to middle class and could not afford to reside in this place. The residents were the upper middle class, a notch higher, but higher nonetheless. They were full of airs better suited to the upper class: the rich. The latter would never dream of putting one of theirs in such an establishment. No, staff would be expected to come to or reside in a wing in their sprawling house partitioned off from public view, where the ailing relative, considered an embarrassment or raving mad or both, was treated like a pariah and spoken of only in hushed tones.

Of course the residents were worse.

The previous home I worked in wasn't quite the Victorian mental institution, but it wasn't far off. Supervision was lax. You weren't quite left to your own devices, but if you thought a resident needed a terse word or a brusque handling then it was always justifiable. So it was possible to let off a small fissure of steam.

When I'd first arrived there I'd been sympathetic to the whining. The inmates were bored out of their skulls. Many sat about listlessly for hours on end, jaws hanging, eyes empty. Some of them pestered strangers – arriving or departing visitors – to wheel their wheelchairs somewhere or simply sit and talk to them. They were ghosts of their former selves, practically fading away, minds adrift. I wouldn't be surprised if one or other scriptwriter for those zombie films hadn't found inspiration in just such a zoo. Within a week I was as uncaring as the rest of the staff. Entertainer was not part of the job description.

This place was certainly a step up for me and would look good on my career profile. I had no trouble getting the position: cut-backs and continual staff shortages – it wasn't the best-paid job – airbrushed any rumours concerning my previous employment. I still had two more weeks of my probationary period to go. After that, it wouldn't matter if they got wind of what I did.

Here, such behaviour would get you a warning. Two warnings were all one would get, said the boss at the interview. Like in some American states where they have that three-strikes rule. Get caught committing a crime a third time, no matter how trivial and they buried you.

We're expected to breeze about with a skip in our step adopting a jolly sing-song not-a-care-the-world isn't-life-wonderful persona, like a frenetic Julie Andrews in *the Sound of Music*, thinking of her favourite things.

Fruit drops and roses and biscuits and boiled sweets,
Bedpans and whispers and brown sodden bed sheets,
Playing at angels with broken wings,
These are a few of my favourite things.

Yes, I have a soft spot for musicals. I know they're not everyone's cup of tea. But they're so clever. Not like an ordinary film where you just got the story. With musicals you got a story and words set to music too. My all-time favourites were *West Side Story* and *Hair*, to name but two. Coming in second place were *Tommy, Evita and Jesus Christ Superstar*.

The residents here, despite their wealthy past and hoity-toity upbringing, were no better than the inmates of my previous workplace. It's just snobbery, a class thing. One could say, that when the facade dropped the contrast was so striking, that they were worse.

Here too were the screamers, the moaners, the snivellers, those that soiled themselves. There were worse in another part of the building, where the poor sods didn't know who or where they were and couldn't dress or feed themselves or anything. Either they were vegetables and you got little out of them or they were belligerent, fighting you every step of the way. As soon as possible this latter lot were shipped off to a mental home, if they didn't pop off first. Luckily, I didn't work there. I wasn't sure I'd last long. I'd probably lose my rag and tip hot porridge over the first one to give me lip.

The next time I visited Mason I gave in to my curiosity. Maybe it was possible to have a conversation with him.

I swept in to take away his breakfast tray and said: "Good morning, Gregory. I'm still here. I'm still alive."

He looked at me queerly, as if he'd not understood what I'd said.

"Have you finished with your tea?"

His brow furrowed as he looked at the half-filled mug, sporting a washed-out photograph of Freddie Mercury and the faded words: "We are the champions." And I smiled as I remembered Wendy taking this cup out of the dishwasher, after we'd been talking about the residents being vegetables and saying: "We are the Champignons."

I gave him a moment before making the decision for

him. "I'll leave it for you to finish."

As I took the mug off the tray to place it on the table he said: "Are more of you alive?"

Now it was my turn to give him a queer look. In his youth he would have been handsome, what they would have called dashing. I could see the ghosts of past mischief sitting at the upturned ends of his mouth line and the crows' feet at his eyes. But overall his demeanour was one of tiredness. He was worn out and appeared to have only two expressions: one that was stern or critical and the other that was blank or bewildered. He was wearing the first, the critical one.

I was poised with the mug in my hand hovering over the table. I put it down. "I should hope so. I wouldn't be able to take care of everyone all on my own, now would I?"

I took his tray to the tall trolley in the corridor and was about to move on to the next room when I changed my mind and stepped back into his room.

"Who do you think I am?"

He adopted his blank expression and thinking he was gone again I made to leave.

"A victim," he said.

"What?"

"A victim."

I smiled and shook my head. "You've got that right." And I left.

Moaning and groaning and endless complaints,

15

We have to take it like angels and saints,
Holding it together with sticky tape and strings,
These are a few of my favourite things.

Later, I wondered what Mason meant. Like many of them here, he wasn't particularly savvy or clued in. Maybe he hadn't been talking generally.

Unfortunately I didn't get the opportunity to visit him again that day.

Until now I may have given the impression that everything works in an orderly clockwork-like fashion. Yes, there is a routine. But that's just a loose framework of administering medicines, washing and dressing, serving breakfast, collecting breakfast, serving late morning coffee or tea, taking lunch and dinner orders for those remaining in their rooms – a consequence of covid isolation, with many of them preferring to be alone – and later serving them lunch and wheeling others to the cafeteria, collecting them later and then the trays from the rooms, offering afternoon refreshment, biscuits, snacks – usually light like a plate of chips or salad or sandwiches – collecting trays again and then helping some with their toilet and getting them into their pyjamas and helping them into bed.

So much for the blueprint. Now, the warts and all.

Dolores wanders about the corridors and needs to be guided back to her room. She doesn't know where she is or who we are, but you can talk to her and she's polite and

16

obedient and allows you to escort her back to her room. We'd love to let her wander about, because she doesn't get in anyone's way, although you've got to watch her when using your fob to unlock the automatic doors and she occasionally goes into someone else's room and stands and stares. She's harmless, but disturbing. Especially when outside visitors are about, we have to coax her back to her room. You see, she wanders about stark naked. She rarely allows us to dress her. It's not a pretty sight, since she's so terribly thin, not quite skeletal, but emaciated with bones jutting white under taut skin.

Edith is the opposite and spends hours in her room. She continually shouts for help, mostly at the top of her voice, until she's exhausted and then in a whiny pitiful voice, until her energy returns. Going to her and asking what she wants is met with "I want to go home. This is a prison. I don't belong here. I've done nothing wrong. Jerry needs his dinner." Jerry was her long dead husband. And her preparing his dinner spoke of a different era.

Phyllis is worse. She actively tries to escape, hovering around the locked doors leading to reception. Once, wearing one of our kitchenette pinnies, she claimed to be a staff member who'd lost her fob to unlock the doors and could we let her out.

My colleague, Wendy, said that we should always double check that we collect all her cutlery after she's eaten.

"She might use a spoon to tunnel her way out." Joking aside, she'd already damaged a window frame with a fork.

Shirley wanders too. She's in the habit of entering someone's room, mainly when they're out, making herself at home and then, when the room's true occupant returns, vehemently claiming it's her room.

These are the exceptions and the majority of the ladies – there are few men – are quite sweet. Their biggest gripe is boredom and lack of company. They would love you to sit and stay in their rooms for a natter. They tempt you with sweets from the tins and bowls they have out. Yes, during the making of a bed or tidying up you chat with them. And the snippets they impart add up to a past life and a sense of melancholy through its passing.

We try to put them together as often as possible. But any friendships are fickle and sometimes degenerate into catty gossip and back-stabbing.

We have an onsite hairdresser and activity centre – similar to a gym, with bicycles, parallel bars (to assist walking, rather than fancy gymnastics), hand weights and a couple of exercise machines. Both are by appointment only. The hairdresser is only present on certain days, but Scott, our fitness trainer – an absolute dish, but well out of my league – is with us mornings. Often we have to take residents to these places and collect them later.

Many can't shower themselves, because they can't

stand for long or don't have the confidence to stand on a wet floor. They have to be bathed. Not only must we get them to the bathroom, we have to help some of them in and out of the bath, which may require using the crane (it resembles a hoist mounted on the prongs of a forklift) – which we also use to help some of the bulkier ones who've fallen. Exercising a couple of times a week for fifteen to thirty minutes, is not enough to keep off the pounds many of them put on in here.

There are the continual niggling requests from the incapacitated. Can you pass me that tin, get me my slippers, read this letter for me and find my watch or glasses? One of us has to collect their post from reception and then distribute it.

Then you have the visitors, friends or relatives, wanting the best for their loved-one, voicing complaints or improvements. I tend to pass the buck, saying they should speak to the duty boss or one of the kitchen staff, or tell them I'll pass the message on. All this delivered with a cheery smile, skip in my step and ingratiating servitude. If they're in my favour they might get a biscuit or cake with their cup of coffee or tea. Extra refreshments and nosh mean extra work for us.

Finally, add shift-work to the mix and you're left struggling to get your life back. Earlies, lates and nights meant you're knackered most of your free time. Social life? That's a laugh. On average, I reckon I have a big night with the girls about once a month.

Boyfriend? Fat chance.

Mason liked his door closed or just a fraction open. Whatever. Before opening it I always imagined him sitting on his throne staring blankly at it. Maybe he was willing it to open? So I was surprised when I pushed back his door with an elbow, tray in hand, and he was not sitting in his chair.

A few times a week he made the effort, donned his tweed jacket as if he was leaving the building, and pushed his wheeled walker all the way to the lounge. He'd had a stroke, which had paralysed his left leg and he lugged it zombie-like. He could walk short distances and his mentality was relatively unaffected. Although, the onset of dementia was showing itself with increasing frequency. Then, this place was enough to turn anyone vacant. His journey to the lounge was akin to a Mount Everest climb, and he stopped at stations to acclimatise and catch his breath. Once in the lounge he planted himself in a comfy chair and read the broadsheets. I think he attempted a crossword too, but rarely finished. Either he lost interest or they were too difficult or he'd phased out.

I heard him in his bathroom.

I set his tray down on the small table and called out: "I've brought your breakfast, Gregory."

The door opened and he stood there leaning on his walker.

"Okay?" I said.

He wore his pyjamas and his annoyed expression. He

pushed the walker on its castors a short distance and then shuffled his right leg forward, dragging his gammy left leg after it.

"Must it be you?"

"What?" I said, before the words: "I beg your pardon" came to mind. I was picking up such phrases from the others here. "Charming, I'm sure," came from the boss. Her air of pretention choked me and I often had the urge to give her a slap, if only to muck up her meticulously applied demeanour.

He continued to move into the room, but I held my ground. Although I wasn't in his way.

"Gregory, just who do you think I am? And don't say victim."

He didn't answer and just shuffled towards his chair and his breakfast tray.

"What's my name?" I asked, making ready to leave.

He then stopped, and looked at me with his blank expression number one.

"If you don't know, I can't help you."

He'd faded out again. I rolled my eyes and stormed out.

Just skin and bone or fat blobs of dough,

Talking of death and feeling quite low,

They are all experts at plucking heartstrings,

These are a few of my favourite things.

Someone else collected his breakfast tray and later delivered morning tea. But I was given the duty of taking lunch and dinner orders.

What would you like for lunch? And you'd reel off the choice of three mains and they'd ponder. Then they'd ask what the first one was again? You'd then list the sides. And the special wishes could come through: no big potatoes and mushy peas not peas, dear – as if they couldn't mush peas with their fork. Sometimes it took a good five minutes to take one order. You had to go to every room and if one was empty you'd have to check whether they were at the hairdresser or in the gym or out with a relative, hopefully having left a message about whether they'd require lunch.

Mason was in his chair when I opened his door. He stared straight at me.

"Hallo Gregory. I'm here to—"

"You're Alison Fielding."

"Alison who?" My pen hovered over the notepad.

He didn't answer.

"My name's Mo."

I ignored his angry number two expression and launched into what he could have for lunch.

Funny how most of them had presence of mind to choose what they wanted to eat. When their meal came a couple of hours later, some had forgotten what they'd requested and complained. Lump it or leave it, was my attitude.

Under his order I wrote the name Alison Fielding. I

couldn't be bothered asking him whether it was Alyson or Alison.

I forgot all about it, until a few evenings later, when I was at home, completely wasted, with the telly on and the sound turned down, waiting for my programme to start, I idly played with my phone. I wasn't big on social media, averaging fifteen hours or so a week, because you weren't allowed to play with your mobile at work. Actually, you weren't allowed to get caught using it. Like the others, I snatched a few minutes with it on the toilet and during my breaks. I hated spending too much time liking this and commenting on that, only to find it was bedtime and another day would dawn. But I did. I knew all too well social media did not equate to social life, but I couldn't help it. I knew the morsels of superficial gratification it gave me couldn't fight my growing dissatisfaction with it. But again, I couldn't help it. Morsels were better than absolutely nothing.

I lived alone in a bedsit. I didn't have any family as such, only a Gran from my mother's side. My father had left my mother for another woman when I was very young and according to my mother had disappeared off the face of the Earth. I never knew him and he never made contact or sent money or anything. I don't blame him for leaving her. As soon as I could, I left her. Stupid cow.

I didn't learn anything from her, other than sewing. Cooking would have been great. Like her, I could only do simple dishes and staples that any bachelor could do. So, I didn't eat particularly well – on this wage I couldn't afford to be choosey about what to buy: cheapest was best. I wasn't fat, but a little on the heavy side for my liking and my skin wasn't good. I knew cheap food contained a lot of fat and salt – but it was so tasty. And don't get me started on wine gums and jelly babies. At work, heavy make-up was frowned upon. I couldn't lard it on like when going out with the girls. The boss made that perfectly clear in the interview. So, I had no chance with Scott or even that new spotty lad in the kitchens.

I searched for "Alison Fielding" and got millions of hits. I guess the search engine looked for Alison and Fielding separately later on. I scrolled down, but nothing grabbed my interest. It was just the usual appalling multitude of social media profiles and personal websites screaming for attention.

My soap started and I put my phone down. I guess subconsciously I continued to think about it, because in the commercial break I found myself entering: "Alison Fielding victim." There were a number of entries on the first page: "Alison Fielding – murder victim". Many of them were Press websites.

I clicked into a reputable site and became so engrossed I missed the beginning of my soap. I admit I can't resist a juicy true crime story.

Alison Fielding had been raped and strangled in Glasgow some thirty years ago – before I was born. She was the fourth victim of the so-called "Cotton-wool" killer. That is, if you don't count his first victim, who survived the attack. The killer's M. O. – short for modus operandi, meaning how the killer operated – was to hit girls walking alone at night on the back of the head. He would drag them into nearby bushes, stuff their mouths with cotton wool, rape and then strangle them. His first victim, the sole survivor, despite a mouthful of cotton wool, had managed to call out and a passerby had come to her aid. The killer fled. The girl said she had not heard him and thought he might have been waiting in a parked car. It was dark and she didn't get a look at him. Her head hurt. When a second girl was attacked and the killer successfully raped and murdered her and it was confirmed that she too had cotton wool in her mouth, the Press started calling him the "Cotton-wool" killer. The public details were necessarily scant, with talk of blunt force trauma to the head, rather than specifying a particular tool or weapon. I also read about small cuts on each of the dead girl's neck or chin, consistent with a sharp instrument, such as a knife. Collected DNA brought no matches on the national databases. In later reports I read that Interpol had not found a match either.

A reward of £10,000 for information leading to the apprehension of the killer was put together by a collective of newspapers. I wondered whether it was still valid.

Looking at a poor quality picture of Alison Fielding, I could see no resemblance to me. Yes, she had dark hair, but that was as far as it went. Well, that's what I thought.

I skimmed over the second, third, fifth and sixth victims because I was getting tired.

As inexplicably as the killings had started, they suddenly stopped. The killer was never caught.

I had made ready for bed, when it occurred to me to search for Mason himself. I was bushed, but I knew I wouldn't sleep unless I looked him up.

I knew he wasn't from these parts. He wasn't a big talker, but I'd never detected so much as a trace of a Scottish accent.

Gregory Mason, including Greg Mason, also got millions of hits. I didn't recognise a younger version of him in any of the photographs and couldn't find a suitable entry within the first five pages. If he had at one time had a website the provider would probably have removed it as soon as his payments ceased.

I didn't sleep well that night. At one point I woke up and searched for "Alyson Fielding victim" on the Internet. But nothing jumped out at me.

Could it be? Could the old fool in his demented state be unwittingly revealing that he was the Cotton-wool killer? Maybe he'd just taken an interest in the case at the time? Yes, of course. But what if?

I was on earlies – six in the morning till two in the afternoon – and I was dead beat before I started. The first thing the shift leader gets me to do after our briefing with the nightshift was the weekly fumigating. That's what we called it. Basically you had to go round spraying odour eliminating spray from a can. You had to do it in a rush in the residents' rooms, because some of them didn't like it. Tough. I was in and out so fast I often didn't catch their complaints. We'd never win this odour war, for the place held the intoxicating levels of a perfume department for about thirty minutes only. Also combating the stench of decay, faeces, urine and despair was a floral insipidity of furniture polish, and disinfectant. None of this won for long.

Then she had me giving the artificial flowers – very realistic-looking with plastic stems and fabric leaves and petals – in the corridors and communal areas a wipe.

Many fine furnishings lifted the home from the hospital aesthetic. Yes, the home was functioning and utilitarian, but it was not scrubbed-down and sterile. With its automatic doors only opening for those with an electronic fob, it could be regarded as a prison. Despite the twee countryside paintings and Laura Ashley patterned curtains, some of the residents believed they were in prison. I'd say the place resembled a proverbial gilded cage. Proverbial. Isn't that a great word? I once overheard one of the residents say it in the cafeteria. I wonder what it means. I'll have to look it up sometime.

As usual I was run off my feet. The one advantage of this was that by the time I saw Mason I had my question honed down to such sharpness, he could not avoid answering it. Well, not unless he'd phased out.

"Afternoon Gregory," I said. "I've come to give you your medicine." I meticulously put his pills together and filled out the date and time on the chart before signing it with my initials.

I approached him with the plastic cup of tablets.

"Gregory," I said and he looked up, his expression undecided: blank, but I thought enquiring. "You said I was Alison Fielding. Are there any other victims here?"

Blank. He'd phased out. Damn it.

"Give me your hand." I tipped the tablets into his palm and poured some more water into his glass.

Some were pickers: taking one tablet at a time and swallowing them individually. Others, like Mason, put their palm to their mouth and took them all at once.

He handed me the glass when he'd finished and I asked him, conspiratorially, a different question. "Alison Fielding was murdered, wasn't she?"

Nothing. He was well and truly gone for the moment.

And that was that for almost a month. I tried again a couple of times, but eventually gave up. I had thought to confide in Wendy, but without more, I could sound as potty as the geriatrics here.

One day I was in Dorothy's bathroom cleaning her dentures – not a pleasant duty – when one of my colleagues,

28

Iris, burst into the room. "Come quickly," she said.

"What is it?"

"It's Gregory. He's in a state."

I wasn't sure what "in a state" meant and, because his room was only three doors down, I didn't have time to think about it. I hastened after Iris.

I heard Gregory shouting well before arriving at his room.

"Leave me alone. You're dead. Get out."

A distressed young girl, in her teens, was standing near his door in the corridor. "I went in the wrong room. I'm sorry. I've not been here before."

"Who are you visiting?" asked Iris.

"Madge. Marjorie Piper. I'm her niece."

"Room fifteen," said Iris, not breaking her stride. "That way."

"I didn't do anything," the girl pleaded. "Is he going to be alright?"

Neither of us replied.

Iris entered his room first and took the stance of talking loudly over his shouts. He wore a very agitated version of expression number two. Strangely, he was in his wing-backed chair, gripping the armrests as if strapped to them, his fingers curled into the fabric, turning and twisting in a taut agony akin to electricity coursing through his body as if he were being executed in an electric chair.

29

"Gregory. Gregory. Calm yourself. Calm down. What in Heaven's name is wrong with you?" She was beside him, trying to look into his eyes. But he was all over the place: head turning this way and that, eyes darting everywhere and nowhere.

"I'll get the nurse," I suggested, thinking she may be able to shoot him a tranquiliser. Or just shoot him.

My voice stopped his thrashing about and he stared at me. "You. You."

Iris looked over her shoulder at me.

"Yes. It's me, Mo– Morag."

"No. You're Alison Fielding."

I glanced at Iris and shook my head pitifully.

"I'll get the nurse."

"He seems to have calmed," said Iris.

And yes, he was still and I could almost see expression number one wash over his face.

Iris turned back to him. "Are you going to be good now? We can't have this carry on, you know. Now, how about a nice cup of tea?"

He didn't say anything, but Iris took that to be a yes.

"Mo?"

I nodded and left the room for our kitchenette. There I boiled the kettle and fetched a teabag. It wasn't teatime so it'd be a bag in the cup.

Dementia is a funny thing. Mason had the presence of

mind to nod when I placed the cup on the table in front of him. And he didn't attempt to touch it when I told him it was too hot.

A couple of hours later I happened upon the girl and an older woman, I took to be her mother.

"Is he alright now?" the girl asked.

"Yes, he's fine."

"I didn't do anything. Honest. I just went in his room accidently."

"Don't worry about it."

But she evidently wanted to tell me the full story.

"He pointed at me and said: 'No, you're dead.'"

This stopped me in my tracks.

"Oh? Did he say anything else?"

"Yes. He said I was dead. He called me, er, Lauren Banks."

"Bangs," I said.

"What?"

"Lauren Bangs."

"Yes, that's right. How did you know? Was she his daughter or something?"

My mind was spinning. "No, no. Nothing like that."

The girl waited for me to elaborate, but I was too confused. "Don't worry about it. It's nothing to do with you. Sorry, but I must get on."

"Of course," agreed the older woman. "We must too."

Once again thoughts of Mason preoccupied me so much I couldn't sleep, despite being completely exhausted.

Lauren Bangs had been the Cotton-wool killer's second victim. Her name stuck with me because I imagined she would have suffered with such a surname. At school she could have been taunted. One question to her full name would be: does she? Or worse, an answer could be: yes she does, she's such a slag. Whatever, the name stuck with me.

The poor girl Mason had upset had only a passing resemblance to Lauren Bangs. But Mason, in his befuddled state, probably thought it was her.

By morning I decided I should talk to someone.

Wendy was on nights. After the short briefing – always short, because end-of-shifters wanted to get home – and invariably some resident would buzz for help, I escorted Wendy to the door as if I was on an errand.

After hurriedly explaining to her, irritated that my brevity didn't do my research justice, she stopped at the door and turned to me.

"As I see it, Mo, you're either right or wrong. If you're right, I guess you should go to the police – but I'd talk to upstairs first. All I know about him, is what you know. Zilch. What was his job? Has he relatives? Nobody ever visits him. Not since I've been here, anyway. Somebody upstairs may know more." I nodded. Upstairs was synonymous with management, which didn't suffer such a high-turnover. They'd know more. "Like you said, maybe this Cotton-wool chap made an impression upon him at the time. Then, if you're wrong, you'll make a bloody fool of yourself. But you're used to that."

I thumped her on the arm. "I'll think about it."

She opened the door and I thanked her.

To go to the boss or to not go to the boss, that was the question. Going to the police directly, without first talking to the boss, wouldn't do my standing any good. I was a full employee now.

Even if they found out about my misdemeanours at my previous job, they couldn't kick me out. I'd lost my rag with a stupid biddy, who'd been fussy about her bathwater: "I'm not getting in. It's too hot. There're not enough bubbles. Don't use half a bottle. Do you think I'm made of money? Swish the water to make it frothy. Then I'll get in." That was it. I told her to get in on her own and wash herself. I'd be back in twenty minutes to take her to her room. She shouted after me, but I went outside into the rose garden. Eventually someone else saw to her. The boss had words and we confronted the woman together. I was made to apologise, but only after the boss had told her how busy we were and that she should show some consideration. Then there was the time I'd slapped old Herbert for insolence. I got away with that by telling the boss he'd pinched my bum.

The next day I called the boss and asked for fifteen

minutes of her time. She saw me at 11:15. Because she shared an office with two others, we went to the library. Here amongst a wealth of books and magazines, ordered thematically and then alphabetically, we sat down in the two easy chairs, near the desk and wooden hard-backed chair. I had never seen anybody in the library and yet books and magazines were collected and returned and signed in and out in the large ledger. New additions were also labelled and filed. Somebody did the work.

"How can I help, Morag?"

"I'd like to ask you about Mr. Mason." She looked surprised and I guess she expected something like a personal grievance or trouble with another staff member. "Can you tell me about him? His job, relatives, anything."

She shrugged. "I'll ask you why when I've told you what I know. A sister brought him to us a number of years ago. I'll have to check the files for the admission date. I think she lives in Australia or New Zealand. I'm pretty sure she said he was a therapist. Have I answered your question? You look as if I have."

"Therapist, yes, maybe." Had he treated the killer? "That would explain things."

An old joke came to mind, but I didn't have time to smile.

"Okay. So why do you ask?"

I decided to give her something, but not everything.

34

"He thinks I'm a dead girl called Alison Fielding."

"Dead?"

"Yes. I did a search and found that a girl with that exact name was murdered about thirty years ago."

She thought for a moment. "Did he say murdered?"

"No. His word was victim."

For a moment neither of us spoke.

"The mind is a funny thing, Morag."

Either I knew where she was going or I was annoyed with her patronising Morag-tone. Regardless, I decided to spill the beans. I wasn't sure how many of the day to day happenings got back to her. "He got excited a couple of days ago, saying a visitor – a girl – was Lauren Bangs. Both Alison Fielding and Lauren Bangs were victims of the Cotton-wool killer. He killed six within two years about thirty years ago. Then he stopped. He was never caught."

I had her now. After the surprise in her expression had subsided I could see her mulling over options and consequences. Eventually she said: "I'm sure it's something he read or watched on television. Don't worry about it. There's nothing we can do."

"What about the police?"

"I don't think they'd be bothered with the ramblings of someone in his mental state."

"I'm sure they'd be interested in closing a cold case," I persisted.

"Really Morag. I think you've been watching too much television. Did he say he was this killer?"

I didn't answer immediately. "No."

"Exactly. When he does, we can talk again."

I knew that if he had treated the killer he would have been legally bound to tell the police.

The joke, one that'd been told on a girls' night out, was about a therapist. Ever since having a new brass plate put at his door he'd had no clients. Looking at it, he realised why. The engraver had not had enough room for the word. Under the therapist's name he had broken it into two. The brass plate then read: his name followed by the two words "the" and "rapist".

Now, I'm not one of those paranoid conspiracy types, but... Coincidence?

Later that day, when I spoke to Wendy about the conversation, she put the proverbial – that word again – spanner in the works by saying that Mason may have been a children's therapist. I didn't tell her about the joke.

The next time I saw Mason he was sitting alone at a table in the cafeteria. I was collecting the trolley of meals for those eating in their rooms. As usual the women from other tables tried to flirt with him. He took their playful advances gruffly, as if they were goading, rather than teasing him. If he reacted, he'd retort grumpily, but never rudely, so they'd take it good-naturedly and giggle like schoolgirls. Likely this was why he was seldom in the cafeteria and chose to eat in his room.

Yes, sometimes he could be surprisingly coherent, which led me to wonder whether his talk of dead victims slipped out.

Nothing out of the ordinary – I mean the ordinary mayhem, because every day was different and yet the same in that mind-numbing way – happened for quite a few weeks, until I came upon Mason in the activity room. Here a couple of tables were devoted to jigsaw puzzle making, two others for board games, which were shelved at the walls.

I was wheeling Joyce in. She liked a change of scene now and again and enjoyed sitting at the bay windows looking out onto the patch of green with its trees and nesting birds.

Despite Edith yelling for help in her room a little further down the corridor, Phyllis was asleep on the two-seater, probably dreaming she was tunnelling out, or maybe she was out: Steve McQueen racing across undulating fields on a motorbike.

Mason was sitting hunched over the table in the bay window, his back to the door, continuing a 5000-piece jigsaw puzzle.

"Here we are," I said quietly to Joyce, not wanting to wake Phyllis. Joyce smiled and brought an index finger to her lips. I parked her in the bay, just beyond the table and Mason.

"Thank you," she said.

I was going to say something along the lines of: "some company for you, Gregory," but he was turning a piece in his fingers this way and that over an area of the partial picture.

Mason must have thought we had lowered our voices so as not to disturb him.

"Help me," shouted Edith. "Someone please."

As I turned to leave, Mason muttered: "Superglue always kept them quiet." He didn't look up and remained completely absorbed by the puzzle. It was almost as if he had said it idly, unknowingly.

I smiled to myself and left the room.

Mason's words stuck with me, not because they were funny or cruel, but because he'd said it matter-of-factly, as if it'd slipped out. As the day progressed I obsessed. At first I was preoccupied, but when I realised what his words could mean, I truly obsessed. "...always kept *them* quiet." Them. Who? Who else could he mean but the victims? I had read nothing about superglue, but I'd seen enough films to know the police held back some key piece of information, to distinguish the fake confessors from the real killer. Insider information, they called it. Something only the killer would know. I also knew that a killer often refined his M.O., learning from previous mistakes. Hadn't his first victim escaped by calling out? Using superglue was simply a natural progression.

This had to be it: the clinching piece of information

that would trap him. He was the Cotton-wool killer.

In the toilets I surfed the internet for "Cotton-wool killer and superglue." But there was nothing. And if it was insider information, something only the killer would know, then it wouldn't be in the public domain. Once home I searched more thoroughly. Nothing.

Talking to either Wendy or the boss would be a waste of time. I needed confirmation. The police were unlikely to tell me anything. I was nobody calling the Scottish police. And who would know such details of a thirty-year-old case? Most of the officers involved would be retired or dead. They'd have to retrieve the file to verify it.

On a day off I discovered via the Internet that all Glasgow autopsies were carried out at the Queen Elizabeth University Hospital.

I called and eventually got put through to pathology.

The person who answered sounded young and not very authoritative.

I gave a false name and said: "I'm a writer researching a book on the Cotton-wool killer. He killed six women thirty years ago. Has detective superintendant Douglas MacIntyre called you? No? Oh, he promised he would. Damn. He was a leading detective on the case and was most helpful. I know you can't show me the autopsy reports, but perhaps you could check something for me. Your superior? When's he back. She? Oh, when is she back? Tomorrow? Oh no, that won't do.

Everything's on computer, isn't it? What's your name I'll thank you in the book when it comes out... Is that Steven with a V or P-H?" How deliciously clever I was. "Yes. Look up Alison Fielding. Okay. I want to know whether her mouth was super-glued... You can't tell me that. I understand. Listen, if there's a comment on file saying you can't tell me, say nothing." Silence. "Okay, Steven, I won't forget to cite you in the book. Thanks– What? Oh, I couldn't say. It'd be called the Cotton-wool killer and probably hit the shelves the year after next. You do that. Okay. Bye."

Gregory Mason was the Cotton-wool killer. Bastard.

I then called the Glasgow police and had a lot of trouble at first understanding them – until I kind of clicked into their dialect, not unlike being at a Shakespeare play, which I don't really make a habit of – and then making myself understood. The latter was more articulation than accent. When it was clear that I had information about a cold case, they seemed surprisingly disinterested or maybe it was scepticism. It was impossible to tell over the phone. They took my particulars and agreed to get back to me.

Two days later I got a text on my phone saying they would like to interview me and when would be convenient. I called the number given. It was a local number. Had they already sent somebody down? The detective who picked up sounded weary and bored. He said the Glasgow police had instructed him to interview me. His enthusiasm was underwhelming. I arranged for him to come late afternoon before work – I was on nights – the following day.

The older detective looked about Mason's age. There the similarity ended. He was what I would call a common man of average intelligence, who'd never climbed the ranks. Years of duty had collected under him to raise him to this final position in his career, where he teetered at the very edge of his competence. His language was trussed up with stock phrases and police jargon. Even this wasn't quite enough to completely mask his common nature.

He was tall with a pot belly and strands of hair combed from one side across his bald pate, in complete contrast to his stocky companion, who looked younger than me and may have been a trainee. He appeared embarrassed and apologetic and I warmed to him. But he was relegated to taking notes and a non-speaking role.

The older one wore thick-rimmed glasses and the pair reminded me of the comedy duo *Morecambe and Wise*.

We'd dispensed with formalities and they sat together on the sofa – incidentally also my bed – and I in the easy chair, which I favoured to watch telly. They'd declined the offer of tea or coffee.

"So, miss – sorry, Morag," began the older detective after I'd related the relevant incidents with Mason. "As you said, it's all circumstantial." I made to protest, but his hand gesture arrested me. "Taken together they could add up to

41

something."

I balked at the word: could.

"He hasn't admitted to being the Cotton-wool killer," he continued. "His illness could make taking this further difficult."

"Sorry. I don't understand."

"Are you familiar with the phrase: unfit for trial?"

I nodded meekly.

"However, such decisions are made by my superiors. They have other priorities, such as taxpayers' money."

I just stared at him. I couldn't believe what I was hearing.

"In any case, it's not our decision. The Glasgow police will have to decide how to proceed." He must have registered my disappointment. "I'm sure they'll want to interview him."

"There was something about a ten thousand pound reward – not that this is about the money. I was wondering whether it's still available."

His eyes twinkled and a ghost of a smile twisted his expression. I shrunk.

"You'll have to speak to Glasgow about that."

And that was that. Morecambe and Wise left and I didn't hear anything more until I came to work for my last shift on nights.

Wendy, who was knocking off after lates, told me after the usual shift handover, that the local police had come that afternoon and interviewed Gregory. Most importantly, the boss was livid with me. Not only had she not been forewarned, but also I had not spoken to her before going to the police.

"Did you see the detectives?"

"Of course. But only in passing. The boss hovered about whilst they were in Gregory's room. She asked me whether I knew you'd gone to the police."

"I don't suppose they said anything? You know, whether he is the Cotton-wool killer?"

"No. They didn't say."

"What did they look like?"

"What do you mean?"

"Morecambe and Wise?"

"Morecambe, I suppose. But not Wise. A young, shy-looking chap."

I nodded and told her that they had interviewed me and I had not been impressed.

I had three days off before starting on earlies. On the second day the boss called me at home and effectively gave me an earful. Anything, absolutely anything, to do with the home had to be cleared with her first. A police visit had stirred up her superiors and she'd had to do some explaining. I was to consider this a first warning. Normally, she'd do the person the courtesy of telling them to their face, but she simply didn't want to see me. More than that, she didn't want to hear anything from, or of, me in the near future. I was to keep my head down and get on with my job.

Through the grapevine I gathered that the boss had been asked by the police when it would be convenient to come by. She'd arranged it so that I wouldn't be around to relish any possible excitement. Petty.

Although the boss had said I should remain out of her sight, she sought me out some two weeks later.

"Oh Morag," she began in the corridor, almost matter-of-factly, "the Glasgow police are convinced Mr. Mason is not the Cotton-wool killer." She was almost gloating.

I couldn't believe it. Bloody Morecambe and Wise. If Mason had killer stamped across his forehead, they'd miss it. Comedians.

I guess I sulked for the rest of the day. At some point I went into the activity room. It was empty. Mason was a hundred pieces or so away from completing the puzzle. I took a loose piece and pocketed it.

Rounds of earlies, lates and nights put the police visit well and truly in the past. Most people forgot it. Even the boss resumed greeting me, if we saw one another.

For me it was not over. I'd given up receiving the reward and I even tried to avoid having anything to do with Mason. But this was impossible. I kept my time with him as short as possible, but still couldn't help listening out for some admission from him.

The unfinished jigsaw puzzle had driven Mason to

distraction and Iris had said she'd remove it after it was broken up. I said I'd have a good look for the lost piece, if I found the time. Then I waited until the puzzle was back in the box, before miraculously finding the missing piece on a shelf behind another box.

I told Wendy that, despite the police not pursuing the case, I still had my reservations. She said: "Innocent until proven guilty." Even she, one of the people here I counted to be on my side, had given up. It appeared I was the only one bothered by a murderer in our midst.

Here he was being fed and watered and cared for and those girls were all dead. And what a cruel way to go; to have your life cut so short.

As time passed I mulled over ways to trap him. The opportunity came unexpectedly.

"You're dead," he said.

The situation could be regarded as déjà vu. In a place like this many situations repeated themselves.

"No. I'm not dead. I'm Alison Fielding and I survived."

Confusion encroached his angry expression. "I saw the life leave your eyes."

That was what I wanted to hear. But it wasn't enough. Who would believe me?

"You didn't press long enough. Do you want to try again?" I went closer. "Stand up. Here's your walker."

His emotion was evaporating and I raised my voice.

45

"Come on. You know what to do. Stand up."

The anger returned.

"Let me help you." I extended a hand across his tray table.

He ignored my hand.

"Get up," I snapped.

He gripped the chair's armrests.

"That's it. Up you get."

I nudged the walker to him with a foot.

He pushed himself out of the chair, huffing as he did so.

"That's it."

Shakily he grabbed the handles of his walker.

I stood in front of it, opened my collar and leaned forward.

His hands reached up and when he held my neck a spasm of fear shot through me, but I suppressed the urge to scream. I knew I would have no trouble throwing him off.

"Squeeze," I said. He was still angry, but there was no strength in his hands. I wanted bruising. I wanted proof. "Come on, Gregory."

It was no good. His hands dropped back to his walker and then he half-stumbled half-fell back into his seat. His face was bereft of emotion again.

Had I seen an evil glint in his eye?

"You bastard," I said, quietly.

46

I went into his bathroom and checked my neck in the mirror. There was not a single mark. I was livid.

When I came out of the bathroom he was sitting in his chair with his eyes closed looking serene.

"You killed them, didn't you? You strangled those girls." Did he nod?

Gregory Mason was the Cotton-wool killer and nobody believed me. I wanted justice, if only for those poor dead girls.

Had I provoked him? Too right, I had. The telling thing was how he had reacted. He'd tried to strangle me. He was the killer.

I had another rough night, stressed and wondering what to do. In the morning I still hadn't decided a course of action. Going to the boss or the police smacked of "crying wolf." You know, the fable told at school of the shepherd boy who cried wolf as a joke a number of times to get people to come running. He laughed when they arrived and they left shaking their heads in dismay. Then a wolf really appeared and he shouted and no one came and he was eaten up.

A week later I still didn't know what to do. I resented doing anything for Mason, but I had no choice.

I went into his room to give him his afternoon meds and found the doctor with him. He was giving him his half-yearly check-up. The doctor said he'd administer the medication today. Good, one duty less, I hope he chokes.

A day or two later I again entered Mason's room. At the

medicine cabinet I noted that the doctor had left his dosage unchanged. When medication was changed for whatever reason, we had to monitor the patient more than normal and the doctor returned a few days later to do another check up. This was not the case with Mason. His next check up would be in six months time, unless anything happened, of course.

I despised Mason, hiding behind his bland innocent expression. I hated the way he tossed back his pills. I hated the ring on his little finger. I hated his superior old-gentleman stuffiness.

One morning I arrived to give him his medication and found Liz from the upper floor kneeling at his feet. She was cutting his toenails. I'd been asked to get qualified to do this, but I'd refused. I couldn't get out of cleaning dentures, changing nappies and other unpleasant jobs. However, I could avoid cutting toenails. Fingernails were okay. The toes of many here resembled a bird's claws. The skin was folded, hard and calloused and the nails themselves were no longer healthy and translucent, but dry and milky and tough. Feet were disgustingly ugly.

"Hey Liz, can I give him his meds?"

"Sure Mo," she said, glancing over her shoulder.

I busied myself at the medicine cabinet.

Liz was talking to him. "Now keep very still, Gregory."

I went over with the plastic cup and told him to hold out his hand. As I tipped the pills into his palm, he flinched;

48

Liz said sorry; and a pill dropped onto his tray table, bounced and then rolled off the edge.

"Damn," I said.

"I see it," said Liz. She reached somewhere under the table, amongst the small collection of bags Mason kept near his feet for easy access. "Here."

"Thanks." I took the pill from her, checked it was clean and placed it in Mason's hand. As I passed him his glass of water to wash them down, I said: "That's the important one." It was true. This one reduced his susceptibility to having another stroke. All the others were to counter its side-effects and support vital organs.

In itself the incident was bagatelle, but it gave me a wicked idea, so wicked I immediately dismissed it.

Over the next few weeks, every time I thought about Mason, the idea presented itself. And when I was at home, I thought about it. And then I realised I was thinking about it all the time. Could I be so evil?

I obsessed.

I don't think I planned to do it when I did. Although the idea had plagued my mind, when I did it, it felt on the spur of the moment. I prepared his pills and then pocketed the main one. I tipped the others in his hand, as usual and watched him swallow them and left.

At the earliest opportunity I flushed the pill down the toilet.

49

In retrospect I should have known nothing would happen. I didn't always administer his medicine and missing a pill once had no effect. Sometimes I would give him his pills three days in a row. Often it was potluck. I decided to hold back his pill every time I gave him his medicine, but no more than three times in a row.

This went on for about two months until one day I came in for earlies and heard that Mason had sufferd a massive stroke during the night and had been rushed to hospital. Strangely, I was genuinely shocked. I'd been lulled by the amount of time my action had no effect. I was anxious too. Both emotions translated well into the required sadness and concern for one of our residents.

He died two days later.

I was on my last day of earlies and Mason's sister and her husband were in his room sorting through his stuff. The boss asked Wendy to take care of them. As usual clothes and belongings that the relatives didn't want would be binned, others sent off to charity shops, some distributed here or to become prizes for a tombola we regularly held.

The furniture would be reallocated or left for the new occupant.

Wendy left them alone clearing his room, but around midday she came and fetched me from the staff room.

"Come and listen to this," she said.

"What? What is it?" I said, annoyed at the interruption

in my break. I put my cup of tea down, but snatched another bite of my sandwich.

Wendy didn't answer and I could only follow her to Mason's room.

"Could you tell her, what you told me?" she said to the sister.

She looked over from the open wardrobe and smiled. "My brother was a brilliant psychologist and criminal profiler. They say he had the uncanny ability of getting right inside the heads of criminals. He took on their persona. I think they later haunted him..." She continued to talk, but I no longer heard her.

Alternative ending (for those with a greater sense of righteousness):

Wendy didn't answer and I could only follow her to Mason's room.

"Ah, you're the one who called the police some time ago," Mason's sister said. She was standing at the open wardrobe.

"The doctors were surprised he had suffered such a massive stroke and so suddenly. And so soon after a check up. There'd been no warning signs. No mini strokes preceding this one, as if his medicines suddenly stopped working. I've taken their advice about carrying out an autopsy."

My expression must have given me away. I felt hot, and I may have blanched and blanked out, adopting Mason's expression number one.

"My brother was a brilliant psychologist and criminal profiler. They say he had the uncanny ability of getting right inside the heads of criminals. He took on their persona. I think they later haunted him..." She continued to talk, but I no longer heard her.

A tale of two tennis players
(erstwhile titled "The best man")

(A very short novel)

0. Introduction

The following story set in eighteen ninety-nine is written in homage to Charles Dickens (1812-1870) and leans heavily upon his novel "A tale of two cities". Thus, the language is somewhat antiquated and by today's standards clichéd. Indeed, on occasion the author interrupts the flow of story as an omnipresent narrator, taking you, dear reader, out of the story – exceedingly old fashioned.

1. Game (Recalled to life)

It was the best of games; it was the worst of games; it was the end of an old life; it was the beginning of a new one; it was the death of certainties and the birth of possibilities.

Thus, dear reader, the stage was prepared for an unpleasant, but memorable, afternoon.

From the very outset, unease frosted the air between the two friends at Defarge's Lawn Tennis Club. Whilst changing, they hardly spoke, confining conversation to strained pleasantries and the subject matter to neutralities such as the fine weather.

"We'll be sweating today," said Sidney, taking an ineffectual chip at the icy atmosphere.

Charles grunted, not knowing how to reply and wondering whether innuendo was concealed in the statement, for his friend was the more quick-witted of the two of them.

After leaving the building in their whites: long-sleeved shirts rolled up to the elbow, blazers slung over their shoulders (such was the heat), long flannel trousers and comfortable footwear – Charles in rubber-soled canvas shoes and Sidney barefoot – both carrying chunky wooden rackets like clubs, they were less uncomfortable because they could settle into the acceptable silence of play.

They draped their blazers over the nearby bench, where they also deposited their club-supplied towels.

"It's a scorcher," said Sidney. "You may want to dispense with your footwear too."

"No thanks," Charles muttered, wondering whether there was design behind Sidney's suggestion.

"Suit yourself."

Charles knew the prerogative for setting the tone lay firmly with him. Even the toss of the coin at the net gave him the serve. Rather than engage his friend, he chose silence. Actually, he didn't choose at all, for he made no conscious decision on the matter. He had not planned a particular stance. His attitude was simply the best way for him to react in the situation.

He took the rubber ball[1] to his area of the grass court and waited for Sidney to nod that he was ready. Was he about to speak? Deliver a witty quip, perchance? Charles was in no mind for levity and most definitely not from Sidney.

When he struck that first ball Charles felt his energies channelled and some of the tension leave him. With direction, a pent-up power that had been winding him up for days prior to this meeting was vented in an ace. (Both men opted for the overhead serve, unlike a lot of women, many of whom still played the underhand serve. Of course, this was Victorian England at the turn of the century and the sport was discouraged for the fairer sex, because of their delicate nature.) Charles had only ever accomplished such a triumphal serve on one occasion, in the gardens of a private manor, and Sidney, somewhat unsportsmanlike though meant in jest, had complained of the distraction of spying the ankle under the dress of one of the ladies playing on a neighbouring court.

No such excuses were possible at this club. Defarge's Lawn Tennis Club was strictly men only.

---

[1] Since the beginning of lawn tennis in the mid 1870s Charles Goodyear manufactured the balls.

Charles was determined to give his best friend the game of his life. Although he invariably lost to Sidney, Charles felt invigorated with a peculiar superiority today. The ball was in his court and he was going to make the most of his advantage. This time he'd win. And not just win, he'd annihilate his friend. Charles was aware that his power teetered at the edge of some darkness, some sinister vindictiveness, and he knew he must harness his supremacy, not only to succeed, but also to avoid losing it to mental disarray.

He played like a man possessed. He played like a demon. He caught Sidney completely unawares.

"What the dickens!"[2] cried Sidney, flabbergasted at another ace of a serve by his friend.

Charles won the first set decisively, but by the second set Sidney was finding his feet. Charles's prowess may have ambushed him and that had been his advantage. Doubt plagued Charles during this second set. Had he merely triumphed because he had taken Sidney unawares? Was it possible Sidney had let him win? The very idea sent a hot spike of hatred through him and his serves became vicious in their delivery. He could see his friend was shaken: his bewilderment evident in his blanched face and in the extra

---

[2] Incidentally, the voiced exclamation had nothing to do with Charles Dickens, who'd died only some three decades earlier, for it had been used by Shakespeare in the 1590s (and perhaps earlier) and was equivalent to "What the devil!"

white of his eyes.

Charles's uncertainty affected his game and this second set became an epic. Neither player would give in. Each exchange went on for the deuce of a long time, as if they were playing for the match point. Just when it appeared over, one of them miraculously reached the ball to keep it in play, shocking the other into action. The games were so hard-fought that it seemed unfair that there should be a winner at all.

Sidney took the second set, by a hair's breadth and even conceded: "Unlucky."

Rather than having a consoling effect, Charles took it as a form of gloating and grew angrier. Sidney would not win. He could not win. He didn't deserve to win. He may be his best friend, but he was not better than him. At best he was his equal. Charles was as much a man as him.

Charles took the third set, itself an epic, much the same as the first one. As if Sidney had lulled himself into his old confidence and relaxed, only to find that Charles wasn't going to go under without a damned good fight. Charles was pleased to see his friend's face cloud over with a determination of his own as they launched into the next game. Yes, mate, you're going to have to do better, a lot, lot better, to beat me today.

He was pleased too, that he'd forced Sidney into uncharacteristic silence. He couldn't be his confident, bouncy, happy-go-lucky, joke-cracking self. Wit certainly had no place when you were forced to concentrate on the game.

Charles was staid to the confident Sidney. These were their accepted and expected roles: Sidney the jester, Charles the king. When Charles married Lucy, it had changed little between the men. If anything, marriage caused Charles to drop any vestiges of self-doubt he had in Sidney's company. Whereas Sidney had remained a lad, Charles had become settled and more at ease with himself.

They had a longer break after this set. Towelling the sweat from their faces, necks and forearms, they waved over the member of staff, who'd been quietly walking the courts with a tray of cold drinks.

The sun beat down on the two beaten men as they drank. It was punishing, thinning the air, accentuating the men's gasping for air. The heat sapped their meagre energy and rendered refreshment short-lived.

Neighbouring courts were now empty. Other players, if there had been any, had prematurely cut their play. Such was the heat. Only dogged mad English men would be playing with such vigour on a day like this, and Charles and Sidney were probably a bit of both.

And why indeed were the two men here? It wasn't merely because they played on a regular basis; something of a tradition that complemented their friendship. Borne out of their bachelor days together, their socialising had necessarily adapted to the fact that Charles was married and Sidney had remained single. Why were they so embittered? Ultimately, behind the entire competition was a salvage operation, a desperate attempt to have their marred friendship recalled to life. Both men probably realised when they met that such an endeavour was doomed from the start. Indeed, although no agreement was verbalised, they intuitively knew this would be their last tennis match together.

Neither spoke. There was too much at stake for chitchat. This was the game to end all games. Masculine pride was at play here. Everything that made men what they were was focused on this one afternoon of tennis. Stamina, strength, wiliness, agility, fortitude, willpower and pride, a good measure of pride, were evident.

Charles's confidence may have made him cocky, because in the fourth set he only won the first game, Sidney taking the rest, as if finding his form.

Charles had succeeded in keeping Sidney off-balance. The games, taking on biblical proportions in their tooth and nail grit, neither men willing to concede, had taken a tremendous amount of energy from him.

Everything now hung on the final set to see who would take the match.

They'd been playing for more than two hours and Charles was exhausted. Sidney looked worn out too.

Charles was so tantalisingly close to victory he could taste it. Yet he could not afford to become smug.

Like Charles, Sidney entered the fifth set bereft of energy; his limbs were weak, ligaments rather than muscle conferring motion, his chest heaving for breath it couldn't catch, his mind driven by sheer bloody-mindedness. He would not and could not lose.

2. Sex (The golden thread)

Five weeks earlier Sidney entered the bar and, with only a few tables occupied, chose a corner table with a view of the door. He correctly assumed Lucy would be purposely late, but he didn't want to take any chances, and had arrived half an hour early. She'd be a fish out of water. Indeed, for him, the place was on the very perimeter of his comfort spectrum. He'd only visited the establishment in a rowdy group twice and when taking into account their state of inebriation on each occasion, it didn't matter where they had landed.

Temple Bar was an old fashioned place, with all the trappings of a traditional tavern, situated near a place of the same name where the heads of executed traitors used to be displayed. The establishment was run by a dumpy, jolly, rosy-cheeked Father Christmas of a man called Tellson.

Nonetheless, Sidney had made an impression on the landlord and they had nodded a greeting. The man undoubtedly liked the idea of a better class of clientele. Sidney was most welcome.

Discretion was the byword. He'd suggested the place to Lucy, because it was off their beaten track and certainly well beneath their social circles. The likelihood of bumping into an acquaintance, or word getting back to someone they knew, was slim to non-existent.

Being midweek meant none of his friends, each one an ambitious, apprentice businessman like himself, was likely to appear.

When Lucy appeared at the door, Sidney almost didn't recognise her. Her unaccustomed makeup was heavy and clownish. Sidney shrivelled, for Lucy had a prettiness that demanded little or very subtle makeup. Her attire was poor too. He'd later discover that she'd bought old clothes from her maid on the pretext of attending a fancy dress ball as a woman of disrepute. Not being buxom she'd done her best to push up and present her wares in the generous décolleté. Completing the disguise she'd somehow procured a wig – usually donned by old ladies who'd lost their hair.

Tellson looked at her with a frown. Sidney knew he tolerated women of dubious virtue. He may even have charged a cut from their gains. Apart from such loose women and an occasional serving girl, pubs, taverns and the like were male only. So he would likely not let Lucy in. Sidney drew his attention with a cough and then a nod to say she was with him and to allow her to enter.

Other men sized her up as she made her way to

Sidney's table.

Any awkwardness that first time Lucy and Sidney met in the Temple Bar dissipated under the heat of gushing, frivolous conversation, in complete contrast to the uncomfortable silence of the tennis match with Charles (related above) a few weeks later.

"The journey here wasn't pleasant," she said. "I didn't like the looks I got."

"I'm sure," said Sidney. "Because you look good." Actually, in his eyes she didn't look good. She was trussed up and painted up. All delicateness bashed out of her with a clumsiness that made her ugly.

Yes, they were uncomfortable at the beginning. But the place filled up shortly after Lucy's arrival and the noise of the crowded place spurred them on and they were compelled to talk loudly. The surrounding repartee and joviality were simply infectious.

"I must admit," she later said, "masquerading has an element of fun."

She laughed when she said she had envisaged the rendezvous being a quiet tête-à-tête, impossible in the riotous party atmosphere.

Alcohol was unnecessary for their banter, but it served another purpose. You see, dear reader, their banter not only drowned any seriousness, but also submerged any thought of what they were doing or more truly, what they were going to do. The most obvious taboo subject was Charles, Lucy's husband and Sidney's best friend. Otherwise talk was easy, if not a smidgen nervous. An onlooker would certainly have assumed that here was a couple much in love. Had such a person heard the talk, which was manic and strident, they may not have been so sure.

Apart from skirting the obvious subjects, conversation covered everything and anything. They spoke of Sidney's most recent acquaintance and why she had not been right for him. Sidney, as aforementioned, was a bit of a lad, which wasn't far off from cad, and not because the words merely differed by a letter. Sidney's looks and charm won many women and subverted the strictures of decorum. He was loved by men too, but purely in the platonic sense. He was undeniably one of the lads, his prowess with women admired by his fellows as much as his competence in outrageous revelry.

There was one other subject they didn't broach. In actual fact it was an incident more than a subject and assuredly a blotch on their friendship. Both chose never to address the event, for to do so was to acknowledge it and cause needless awkwardness that could serve no purpose. This was a wound that only time could heal–

To procrastinate further, dear reader, would undoubtedly tax your patience.

The said incident transpired during a ball. Sidney characteristically bounced between eligible maidens, flirting terribly, but found himself at one rare moment sitting out a dance. Charles had disappeared, leaving him alone with Lucy. All three of them were quite tipsy and dangerously close to flouting acceptable behaviour.

Sidney was relishing the party and attention. Other beaus were decidedly grey and boring by comparison. He was talking to Lucy, but in accordance with his disposition, more talking at her than to her, almost oblivious to her presence. Hence, when he momentarily glanced her way, he was caught by the twinkle of adoration in her eye and lingered. And in that ensuing linger he saw enticement. Shock overwhelmed him and he rejected her. He would never steal his friend's escort. (The couple were in their early courting days.) He rode his rejection with hasty banter, but not before he registered her hurt.

And that was the end of it. Sidney took Charles's reappearance as a cue to leap away. He even pretended not to hear his friend's suggestion of asking Lucy to dance.

But let us return to the present and Lucy and Sidney at Tellson's.

"Are you often here?" she asked.

"No. It's not my kind of place."

"But you are familiar with the proprietor."

"I've been here twice. He no doubt remembers me from the last time. I wasn't exactly quiet with the lads." He then launched into a couple of humorous – borderline vulgar –

anecdotes that warmed her to him.

Sidney was a conversationalist, a small-talk veteran. He effortlessly persuaded people to talk and should his encouragement fail, he could quite easily carry the burden of conversation by himself.

Serious subjects were touched upon too. Politics for one.

"I'm glad you chose America, rather than India or Africa," she said.

"I'm steering well away from Africa. This second Boer War has put me off."

"The so-called concentration camps sound horrendous," she said. "I can't believe there's any truth to them." She paused, before suggesting: "Doubtless, propaganda."

Sidney was astonished by her knowledge, for it was not the province of ladies to know of such things. He assumed Charles had told her, but chose himself not to pursue the subject. "India was tempting," he admitted. But here too, he'd heard rumours of nasty acts of suppression.

"But all those dreadful diseases!" she exclaimed. "Typhoid fever!"

He thought of the current famine the country was suffering, but decided not to mention it. The conversation called for an upturn.

"New York, here I come!"

"But you're not staying there."

"No. I'm going west!"

"To fame and fortune," she said quietly, sadness glazing her eyes..

He lifted her phrase with his glass and toasted: "to fame and fortune."

She did likewise, smiling as she repeated the phrase.

"You sounded a mite jealous," he observed.

She laughed easily. "Not in the least!"

He knew she meant it. She and Charles were settled and were not looking for adventure and certainly not the upheaval of emigrating. They were hoping for an adventure of a different kind, that of bringing up a child.

Sidney was grateful for Lucy's attitude. She was a wonderful woman and a perfect fit for Charles. Sidney found her attractive, but there was something motherly about her that he couldn't quite put his finger on. Her attractiveness was of the lasting kind. Sidney was drawn to women who were more sensuous, more obvious with their sexiness: the type of women all men were drawn to, but few could have. And such women knew their beauty and often exploited it. If the exploitation was done with intelligence and aplomb, without too much conceit, then Sidney would be intrigued. Oh, Lucy had fire, but it wasn't as passionate as he liked it. He wanted a good-looking woman who would challenge him, who would box his ears, box him in, but then release him, and yes, be his

66

punch bag too. Basically, he liked women with wayward spunk. Lucy's spunk was of the diplomatic kind.

He knew Charles saw it differently for he had once told Sidney that he, Sidney, liked his women to be on the tarty side.

At a nearby table, food had been served with the tavern's unique cutting device. The sight and sound of a novelty guillotine, practically a children's toy, slicing bread and then various vegetables, followed each time by a roar of delight, much the same as that when witnessing a fireworks display, occupied the couple for some moments.

"Do you think we've had enough?" she asked, glancing at her empty glass and placing her hand on his. It wasn't a question, even a rhetorical question, it was a statement akin to "I think we've had enough." Coming from her, it could only be taken to mean that she had drunk enough. So, it was a question that did not require an answer.

Sidney knew, like her, he had been procrastinating.

The touch of her hand didn't go unnoticed and Sidney waited for her to lift it, before nodding and leaving their table for the bar, where he spoke to Tellson.

Lucy watched as Tellson reached for one of the keys hanging from a board between the shelves of bottles, glasses, tankards and beer mugs. They conversed for a moment, with both of the men holding the key.

Temple Bar was primarily a tavern and not an obvious

whorehouse, but Tellson did rent some of his upper rooms for an hour or two. He didn't tolerate solicitation on the premises, but women from the street could come in with a punter and rent a room.

Strictly speaking, because of the bedrooms, the place was not a tavern but an inn. However, it was testimony to the triumph of its disguise that it was referred to as a tavern.

Lucy refused to entertain the thought that Tellson – and everyone else, for that matter – regarded her as a whore. She couldn't act, and chose to treat the experience as a game. She averted her eyes, lest the proprietor glance her way. She thought she had done herself in the image of the type of girls who attracted Sidney. If a whore, then she was at the very least a courtesan, a high-class prostitute, ones that attracted gentlemen with fat purses.

She was still staring at her reticule (her small fabric purse that she often carried upon her wrist) upon her lap, again admiring the pattern in the golden thread stitching, when she realised someone was standing near the table.

Lucy looked up and for a moment, through a trick in the light, she thought it was her husband standing before her. But it was Sidney. Both men were similar in stature. More than this, both were dark-haired with similar features and many had questioned whether they were brothers, although they were not in the least related.

Asked if she loved Sidney, she would have said yes. She

loved her husband too. She loved both men, but in different ways.

As a character Lucy sat between the two men. She could rise to the challenge of Sidney's scathing wit for a good length of time, but it was an effort to maintain and she was more at ease, and thus herself, with her husband. Sidney was too errant for her. Deep down a part of her felt sorry for him. For she believed he was adrift, but not a hopelessly vanquished sot. Although, stories of his escapades with other lads meant that he could comfortably adopt such a hopeless persona.

With respect to the incident at the ball she was not honest with herself. She told herself that it had not been an offer. Undeniably, it had not been a sincere offer. At that particular moment, like many of the maidens in the room, she had glowed in Sidney's company. Buried in the recesses of her mind, she knew her expression had been a puerile whim to see if he would bite and that was all. Consequently, Sidney's rejection had been more than humiliating; it had been especially hurtful, because he had so obviously taken her frolicsome invitation in earnest.

Lucy looked up at Sidney and was suddenly uncertain. Did he see the apprehension in her eyes? His face was in shadow and she could not tell. He showed her the key, rather unnecessarily, and held out his other hand. She took it and rose and allowed him to lead her through the crowd and up the stairs.

3. Match (The track of a storm)

Lucy knew better than to ask. She merely glanced up from her embroidery when Charles entered the drawing room. He had on what she called his serious face. But it was more than a serious expression. A small (what she called – because it so reminded her of a bulldog) pug of skin appeared at the top of his nose when his brow puckered into a frown. When she first noticed it, and his humour could appreciate the observation, she remarked that she knew when he was worried or angry, because he developed the beginnings of a unicorn's horn.

Despite her reassurances, sometimes exasperating reassurances, she had the feeling she had never completely convinced him that he had nothing to worry about. Now that Sidney had finally left for America maybe the pug of skin would recede and eventually disappear. This ugly disfigurement in her husband's handsomeness was hopefully but a track of a storm of emotional upheaval, a true test of their marriage that was thankfully over.

Or was it over? Lucy worried, but she had to be strong for her husband. She gave no harbour to Sidney's ghost in their bedroom. She knew too, that emphatic reassurances given to her husband could backfire, because of their very

70

vigour.

Although she took leave of her embroidery, holding the framed cloth on the mound of her belly, she did not look at him directly. But she was aware of him standing somewhat forlorn at the mantelpiece, as if he had suddenly found himself in the room and didn't know what to do with himself.

She admired her artistry, comparing it to the picture of the simple house, sun and flower, all rendered with a child's coarse simplicity. She had stitched the pictures and now the word "Bless" of the phrase "Bless this house". She contemplated showing it to him, but then decided to let him speak first.

Lucy would have liked to have seen Sidney off. The doctors had advised rest and partaking in a Hansom cab ride over cobbles and the like was not deemed prudent. Therefore, Charles alone had gone to see his friend board the mail coach that would take him to port. She had seen him only once since her announcement seven months ago and that was merely a few days ago to say goodbye. Her husband had been out of the house at the time.

She had met Sidney in this very room. As far as the servants were concerned he was family and so leaving her alone with him raised no eyebrows. He had also stood awkwardly near the fireplace, although it had not been lit, and claimed that he could not stay because of an impending engagement. The two men were so alike.

"We shall miss you," she said, watching him from her chair.

He nodded and smiled, uncharacteristically at a loss for words.

"I shall miss you," she added.

The statement only served to plunge him deeper into reticence.

Did he miss their rendezvous? She missed the delicious naughtiness that they eventually took on. Dressing up and pretending had been fun: fun that required harnessing.

She wished that he would stay for the birth, but knew that he was decided and that it was probably for the best.

"Whatever happens," she continued, trying to put him at ease, "we hope you find happiness."

"I know," he managed. Then he lifted his timepiece by its chain from his waistcoat and clicked it open.

The action made her desperate. It all seemed so inadequate and she so wanted to reach him. "We love you," she said, suddenly. "Charles loves you." He pocketed his timepiece, still unable to look her directly in the eye. "I love you," she added.

He smiled and looked at her sardonically. His expression was unexpected and puzzled her.

"I love you too," he said unemotionally. "I love you both."

He moved to leave and she stood. Then he approached

her and held her by the shoulders and kissed her on the cheek and said: "Farewell, Lucy."

This wasn't enough for her and she hugged him and he let her do so.

They disengaged, smiled awkwardly and he left.

Lucy was amazed at how primitive men were in their emotions. They may be intelligent and logically superior – the suffragists would disagree – but they were cavemen when it came to emotions; as simplistic and readable as her needlework.

Her husband had been in a dreadful state for too long. She worried terribly he would lose his head. Even now, now that Sidney had departed, he was trying to become a unicorn.

She had thought the men would be reasonable: stiff upper lip and that sort of thing. Instead, their friendship was ruined and her husband, especially her husband, suffered. He tormented himself. Lucy couldn't understand his obsession with something as nebulous as manhood and she suspected he didn't fully understand it himself.

His one proud moment in all these months appeared to be winning (by a whisker) a silly game of tennis with Sidney. And from what she gathered neither player had enjoyed playing. The more snippets she received over time, the more it sounded like a bitter encounter. They never played again. In fact, they had not met until this very day: the day of Sidney's departure.

Charles readily admitted he was in a state. By turns he was strong and gruffly annihilating, and then weak and vulnerable. Whatever state he was in, was precarious and if it endured, he hated himself and tore himself out of it with such verve that he ended up at the opposite extreme; equally unsustainable. Lucy told him again and again that she was in no danger of her falling for Sidney. And no, physically he was not better than him.

Charles and Lucy had been trying to have a baby for four years when they began considering adoption. All available tests said that she could conceive. Contracting mumps as an adult had rendered Charles sterile.

Then an article appeared in the paper, in which an adopted child had grown into a youth, only to return and murder his adoptive parents. This news caused the couple to hesitate.

When Sidney announced his intention to emigrate, the idea was hatched. Whose idea it was is unclear. Charles remembered voicing the suggestion, but had it been at the subtle behest of his wife? It was a mute point, for although Charles was uneasy, he agreed, without fully understanding the consequences. Certainly, it wasn't the topic of manly, after-dinner brandy-and-cigar conversation.

Charles went to the brandy decanter and poured himself a good measure and returned to the fire. He recalled their stifled conversation, more interlocution, before Sidney climbed aboard the coach.

"It is a far, far, better thing that I did," Sidney began, evidently having prepared a speech of sorts, "than I have ever done; it is a far, far, better to go west, than to stay here near your home."

He promised to write. Indeed, they would receive a letter from him to say that he had arrived safely and was preparing to head west. And that was the last they heard from him. They never received the opportunity to reply. So they could not deliver news of the birth of their bonny daughter.

Both Lucy and Charles would find sanctuary in the child, whose innocent love would dwarf the wedge in their relationship. Years later they would have a period of rejuvenation in the bedroom and Charles's pug of skin would truly disappear.

The downturn in the men's friendship was regrettable and irreparable. It was also painful for both men. So much so that as they made their farewells neither of them could speak of it.

"I thank you, my friend," said Charles. "I am sorry."

They shook hands and then, as if to acknowledge Charles's last words, Sidney hugged him. Then he turned and stepped up to board the coach, stopped, as if he'd changed his mind, and made one more remark, also rehearsed, which left Charles rooted to the spot. This he related to Lucy when he began haltingly talking of seeing their friend off.

"I was nearly too late," Charles said. "He was the last to board. All the bags had been stowed." He took a good gulp of brandy.

"I thanked him and..." He had trouble continuing. "I apologised." He fell silent, staring into the fire.

"And... as he climbed aboard... he said..."

She waited, but he seemed to have drifted off.

"Pray tell," she prompted, gently.

He looked at her bewildered. Then his face cleared as if he remembered what he wanted to say.

"He said: Greater love hath no man than he lay down his wife for another."

Buddies

Brac would say that the hallucinations started after he was struck by lightning. Duh, what were the odds? He hadn't even been on the highest roof of the building. There were two above him, also flat with a low parapet like this one. They were set back like a further block of a building each smaller than the one upon which it sat. The silhouette resembled a block pyramid or short flight of steps. He was not on the lowest roof either. This one gave him a perfect view of the target: a balcony of a neighbouring building some two hundred yards away. His roof elevated him above the level of the target balcony. Any higher or any lower and the balconies above and below would reduce the target one to a slit. His position presented the best possible shot, which under normal circumstances would have been relatively easy. But heavy rain and strong winds had turned the hit from routine to difficult. The premature darkness too meant that he had to work with shapes.

When he had set up, the rain had been torrential, a veritable tempest, lightning and all: the end of the world – biblical. The overhead river of clouds moved, low, in a rapid flexing swiftness that was almost living. Then the rain became heavy, big drops of water, hard as hail, pelting his head through his flat-cap. His Homburg would have offered some space and spared his head, but his dark, beret-like cap with its marginal brim was more practical for such work. Now the rain had eased off to a light drizzle, giving him better visibility.

His thick Crombie was soaked and hung on him like a wet blanket. A sou'wester and complete oilskin would have been more appropriate, but the material was reflective and could give away his position. He wore nothing reflective: no jewellery, no adornment, not even a timepiece. He also carried no identification. He did have an untraceable Saturday night special in one pocket and slugger, his knuckleduster, in another. He preferred them over knives. He hated knives: too messy and unpredictable. A gun allowed you a modicum of distance and slugger fitted so firmly, you would have to pry it off.

The building was derelict, the roof in disrepair and completely waterlogged. So he had chosen to sit on his haunches away from the parapet at the wall to the building, watching through his binoculars. Sometimes he stood, but then his view of the balcony was slightly obscured. The wall afforded him some cover from the rain. His rifle lay at the ready, but looked abandoned, the telescopic bipod resting on the edge of the low parapet. Brac's legs suffered most, because the rain water did not drain off the flat roof quickly enough. His thighs and calves were like blocks of ice, stiff and threatening to cramp.

Brac was tough – as tough as they came – and a little

water was not going to stop him from fulfilling his task. The job was simple: take out the rival boss as soon as he came out to smoke his cigarillo.

Some bosses wives wore the trousers at home, but only at home. This was the case with his target. His wife insisted that he smoke outside.

Should the wife also come out, he was to take her out too. So he was to wait a moment after taking down the boss, in case she should appear. No children were involved, but if there had been, he would have had no qualms about killing them too. He had heard the World War Two story of the two German soldiers in the firing squad detail, in which one shot the parents and the other their children, the latter justifying his action as a mercy killing, sparing the children lives of hardship as orphans. That's exactly how Brac reasoned it, except that he was both soldiers rolled into one. Any regret he may have felt for each victim was satisfied with a candle and a twenty in the church collection tin. A true career criminal could not afford the luxury of a conscience. Period.

He had counted off the floors and knew the position of the room.

Although the curtains at the glass doors to the balcony were drawn, light glowed where the upper pleating didn't meet the edge of the window frame. The room was occupied.

Whilst the storm had raged the boss had been unlikely to come out, which was fortuitous for Brac, because merely wounding the target would mean failing to complete the task. Now that it was reduced to a drizzle he would surely want to have a smoke before the weather changed for the worst again. The clouds remained broody. Flashes of distant lightning, hot phosphorous-white roots shooting down from, and lighting up, the underbelly of the roiling charcoal and grey mass, followed by the long tumbling rumble, meant the storm was far from over.

There was one advantage to the weather: any evidence would be washed away.

Two hundred yards meant he didn't need to compensate much for the wind, which wasn't as strong as earlier. Frenchie would propel her projectile straight and true to drill right through wherever he pointed her. These were the best kind of jobs, with no intimacy, no contact and no chance of transference. The hit was no more than shooting a moving tin duck at a carnival. This was a headshot. There was the uncertainty of missing a vital organ with a body shot. An order to wound for a slow death was a hit in the stomach. Maiming could be a shot in the jaw, elbow, kneecap or ankle. With a kill Brac invariably aimed for the head which exploded like a blown-up beefsteak tomato. That's a hit.

So he waited on the roof in the wet and cold and dark, staring through his binoculars, focused on the balcony. He imagined the boss coming out and lighting up. In the instant his face was illuminated Brac would squeeze the trigger. He would be dead before taking that first drag. Huh, maybe his cigarillo would hit the floor unlit.

As a boy Brac had learnt patience, by spending many a silent hour perched up in a tree stand with his father, waiting for deer or boar. His father had taught him how to shoot: relax your breath, focus your mind, squeeze – don't pull – the trigger. His father had shown how to care for weapons: treat them with respect and they'll do you good service. Give them a name, if you want. His Frenchie was a French snipers' weapon, an FR F1, bolt-action rifle. She had never let him down. His father had told him that the waiting could be meditative: a time to step back from the hectic world. He merely had to suspend himself: give himself up to the time.

His father had been stocky, whereas Brac had grown to be a big man. Some called him a big lug. And yes, his rifle was like a toy in his big hands. However, his lumbering size belied a gentleness obvious in the way he treated and held Frenchie. When he cleaned her, he did it with the utmost affection.

The curtain moved: a spike of light appeared and then disappeared as it fell back into place.

Brac got up, pushing his binoculars deep into his coat pocket, and hastened in a crouch to Frenchie. He lay down carefully, legs spread and lifted her wooden butt-stock to his shoulder, nestling her there like the head of a girlfriend. His index finger sat on the trigger guard, while the rest of his hand clasped the handle. His jowls lay on her padded cheek rest as he peered through the telescopic sight that he had focussed earlier.

He too was focussed and thus oblivious to the rain patting his flat cap, immune to the water soaking up from the roof into him and unaware of the cold devouring his legs.

The rain wasn't heavy and the sheltered balcony appeared relatively dry. Now was the time to come out and take a smoke. Surely–

A phosphorous-white light cauterized all further thought.

When he regained consciousness little appeared to have changed and he surmised he had only been out for a few seconds. He was still in his prone position, but now on his back with his coat and jacket open. The balcony was still dark and empty; the rain was now drizzle and fading to mist. Frenchie was gone. She must have fallen over the edge when he was struck. By far the most significant change was in his head. He felt as if somebody had walloped him with a hand axe. The pain was excruciating. His eyeballs felt as if they were about to pop out of their sockets. The pain was so bad he tore off his hat and throwing it like a Frisbee, grabbed the sides of his head with both hands. This brought him nothing and he rose to his feet and staggered blindly about, all the while clutching the sides of his head as if he could somehow squeeze out the pain.

Had lightning hit the back of his head? The top of his

head felt delicate and he daren't touch it. Or had lightning struck the roof somewhere else and this searing pain was the effects of electrocution?

It didn't matter. He couldn't really think about it. In fact he couldn't think: the pain was all-consuming. He was screaming for relief, but nothing helped. His eyes were shut tight. He was cold too. Some primordial instinct for survival kicked in, and buttoning his jacket and coat, he lurched away from the edge of the building.

His gait was also uncomfortable because he had soiled himself. Did being struck by lightning empty the bowels? Boy, did he stink. In addition there was stickiness at his groin. Was ejaculation a result too?

He had to get home and take some Aspirin and clean himself up. The boss would be disappointed that he hadn't made the hit, but under the circumstances...

Brac remembered nothing of the journey home. When he got to his flat his headache had subsided. He should have taken aspirin and cleaned himself up, but he was too cold and tired and just crashed on his bed. His jacket and coat were unbuttoned and he did them up. Didn't he do that on the roof?

"Hey Brac," said Jimmy. "He'll pay what's due. Lean on him a little."

"Only a little," added the boss. "He's got that gammy leg, from that hammer to the knee, last time."

"Yeah," said Jimmy, chuckling. "He might just fall over."

The two men had laughed and Brac had allowed himself a smile.

He awoke feeling icy. Although he wanted to sleep, he knew he should take a hot shower. In the bathroom he removed his coat and jacket. When he took off his shirt he noticed that his left underarm was red, as if bruised. His chest above the U of his white vest was red too. He pulled off his vest to see that his upper body was blotched red and white. Yet, in the mirror he saw no such staining. He pressed a reddened area near his stomach and expected pain. Instead, he felt nothing and under pressure the red gave way to whiteness.

He pointed to a red patch and checked the reflection. In the mirror there was no redness. Nothing was wrong with him. It didn't make sense. Was he dreaming?

It was far too cold for a shower. As his father used to say arriving home from the building site, when his mother said he should take a shower, hey, woman, no one died of smell.

If he did take a shower, it did nothing for him. He felt as dirty as before. More than anything else he felt oh so tired. So he unthinkingly dressed and went back to bed.

"Here," the boss had said, taking a thick envelope from his desk and handing it to Brac. "Give that sack o' shit this."

The sack o' shit was a ranking cop. "It's part of our cut from the heist." Brac knew he was talking of a gang's armoured security truck hit, the organisation had sanctioned for a cut. "Those on our payroll get their wages." He smiled. Brac returned his own tight smile. He could see the irony of robbing the cops of their wages and then dishing out to the deserving ones.

The next time he woke, he didn't feel so cold. He was appalled to see that he had donned his sodden clothes. His coat and jacket were open. Funny, the buttons didn't feel loose. Must be the way he was lying. Had he taken a shower? He wasn't sure. The smell was worse. He truly ponged. Maybe he should take one again. But he found he couldn't move his head. Huh, he couldn't close his eyes or open his mouth. It was as if he had lock-jaw. Weird. His neck had seized up too. He used his hands to knead his neck – to no avail. When he went to touch his jaw it wasn't where he knew it should be. His chin was shattered and gone. He gathered his will and tried to move his head, but it would not budge and his anger quickly changed to despair. And for the first time in years, maybe decades, he felt as if he could cry.

He struggled to his feet and shuffled to the bathroom. He was so tired. The mirror showed him his accustomed square jaw and his complete self. Yet, the area about his chin felt ravaged. He couldn't even feel some of his lower teeth and there was something terribly wrong with his tongue. He felt shorter. Try as he might, he couldn't turn his head or open his mouth and so check his tongue in the mirror. Tentatively tapping his fingers up the sides of his head, he found a smashed area near the back. His fingertips touched something delicate and he was reminded of his childhood breakfast eggs in their egg cups. His father always pencilled a face on them and Brac would bash the head in and his father would pick off the bits of shell for him. He couldn't see the back of his head and he didn't possess a hand mirror. He thought of using the kettle, which was shiny and reflective, but he was too fatigued for the palaver of holding it up behind his head and manoeuvring himself in front of the mirror. Besides, he intuitively knew that the reflection would show that nothing was amiss. Anyhow, if he truly had a hole in his head, how could he think? Duh.

He returned to bed. Brac knew patience and his father had always said: if you can't do something about something then eat it up. Yeah, that was what he would do. He would ride it out. He couldn't close his eyes, but he could become sightless. He would numb his mind to vision – the uninspiring ceiling– and he would become unseeing. He would wait.

"Where is she?" asked the boss.

"I left her in the cellar, boss," said Brac.

"You did better than that," said Jimmy.

Brac kept his composure.

The boss's enquiring look was enough.

"I hung her up on a hook on the back of the door." Her jacket had fitted perfectly over the hook. She wasn't going anywhere in a hurry. Maverick hookers were not tolerated on any of their patches, no matter how young, or if they were just starting out with some sob story of being hungry and feeding their hopeless mother's habit. All hookers had pimps. Period. She would come round after a few days.

"See what he did?" said Jimmy to the boss. "He went and hook' her." And Jimmy laughed at his own joke.

When he next assessed his state – it felt like hours later – he found that his predicament had worsened. He could not move his body and his limbs were stiffening too. To move an arm required a gargantuan effort. His legs too. Was he dreaming? Was this sleep paralysis? He knew a mechanism kicked in during sleep to stop your legs moving when you were dreaming of running for instance. He didn't think he was dreaming or that he was even asleep.

Brac was never one for drugs. He had seen too many junkies to become one himself. In truth, he was a little scared of taking them. His immediate boss, Jimmy, the underboss to the boss, snorted. The boss didn't do drugs and Brac modelled himself on him. He even wore a fat gold ring on his left pinkie just like him. He was a dapper dresser too. Okay, his suits were not as expensive and he did not have as many as the boss, but dressing well was a must. He could take being called a thug, but he was no slob.

87

Was this what taking drugs was like? Had someone slipped him a Mickey? When? Jimmy was never like this. If anything he became more animated, wild, unpredictable.

Brac was in the room waiting for instructions as Jimmy explained to the boss what had gone wrong. "I told him to light the lighter when he'd doused him in gas and wait. I guess there was a breeze from them broken windows and the flame was kinda wild and he dropped the lighter and it all went up. Trouble was he'd stepped in the puddle under the chair and maybe splashed himself too, so in a moment he was a torch too. The extinguisher didn't work."

Another time, Brac was also present when Jimmy was explaining a mix-up and how they had rigged the wrong car and some broad, a bottle-blonde, got blown up. "She was a good-looking woman too. A real bombshell."

Brac intermittently assessed himself and found that his state progressively worsened.

Then – it seemed more than a day later – he could move. In fact he could more than move, he felt light as if his entire body was hollow and his limbs flaccid. Contradicting this feeling was his bloated belly. He was a balloon – a balloon filled with water.

His coat especially felt heavy. But he realised that his pockets were empty. The binoculars, his shooter and slugger were gone. His gun and knuckleduster could have fallen out when he rolled over. Had he left the binoculars at the wall?

Although he felt surprisingly weak, especially after so much rest, he sat up and a moment to two later – or an hour or two later (he was no longer sure of anything) – he stood. His Crombie and jacket were of course open, he undid his waistcoat buttons, and then those of his shirt. His belly was almost bursting. What had he eaten? Bowling balls? He certainly felt full. Lifting his vest he found the skin of his distended abdomen was marbled, greenish and black and spotted with what looked like blisters. Touching them he felt nothing. But he noticed his fingernails. He was always particular about keeping them short and clean. They seemed to have grown extraordinarily long. Then maybe the ends of his fingers had somehow receded to make them look long. Creepy.

What the hell was happening? Had he been on that roof? Or had he been here all the time, dreaming he was on the roof? Of course he had been on the roof. He was no loony.

He went to the bathroom again, leaving his clothes open and hanging from him. His innards gurgled and grumbled. He leaked as he walked, liquid trickled and slime edged down the insides of his legs. Did he have dysentery? The stench was appalling too. Gastritis? That would explain his stomach too.

In the mirror he was astounded and relieved to see his true self with normal colouring, not a blister in sight. Even his nails were normal in the reflection. It didn't really help how he

89

felt.

Was he daydreaming? It had never happened to him before. He was not the type to have flights of fantasy and never such bizarre thoughts.

Who and when could someone have slipped him some drug or another?

He would not find the answers in his flat. Of that much he was certain. He loathed the idea of facing his boss and admitting failing to take out the target, but he knew he had to remain upstanding. Sometimes you simply had to face the music, no matter the consequences. Eat it up.

So he pulled down his vest, stretching it over his horribly swollen belly, buttoned up his shirt and then his waistcoat. He only did one button on his jacket and with his heavy coat finally closed, his stature meant that his belly didn't show at all.

The boss was not in his office. More than that, no one was about; none of the guys. There was always someone. The place was never completely deserted.

The two dolls were still in their boxes on the shelf. Dusty now. Mrs. Koska must be ill again. The boss really should get another cleaner. But favours were favours. The dolls were keepsakes from a robbery gone wrong. The guys had stolen the wrong truck. After realising he couldn't sell the hot toys, the boss had them delivered to all the orphanages. Christmas came early that year for a lot of kids. The mayor didn't have the heart to confiscate them and with the toy company he jumped on the good publicity band wagon and claimed it was a joint charitable act. The organisation knew better.

Brac stood for a long while wondering where everyone had gone. The boss had always liked the minimalist look, without clutter like a showroom, but now the office looked lifeless.

Huh, he had been christened in this very room.

He had been in the office with his partner, when Jimmy had brought the boss in all those years ago. Jimmy had furnished the room. But the boss said: "What's with all the bric-a-brac?"

To hide his embarrassment Jimmy had pointed to the guys and said: "You mean Bric and Brac?"

As luck would have it, because of where he was standing, he got the name Brac. His partner got Bric and although it sounded solid and dependable, even without the k it still rhymed with thick. Brac liked his name. The discovery that it was spelt without the k sealed it for him. When asked, he told the boss he wanted to be called Brac, explaining that it was a past tense of broken and that fitted his job description. He liked it without the k, because it made him exotic like a French film star and most suitable when considering Frenchie. He didn't say this to the boss; he didn't want to appear thick or soft: no one knew he had a name for his rifle, like some guys nick-named their penises.

Jimmy had hand-picked him and Bric from under his capos, elevating them to his private henchmen and occasionally beefing up the boss's bodyguard. So Bric and he had been raised above all the soldiers to be directly answerable to Jimmy, the underboss. And their names gave them real identity within the organisation.

Unfortunately Bric got hit a couple of years ago and a new guy, a real empty-headed lug, had replaced him. He *was* a brick with a k – as thick as they came. He was built but did not have any special skill like Brac. He was nobody and didn't deserve a special name.

"Where are you, boss?" Brac asked the empty room. A hint of despair entered his voice, when he said: "Where is everybody?"

The excursion exhausted him and back in his flat he again lay on the bed.

"I want you two to go," said Jimmy to Bric and Brac. "The boss doesn't want no beef with the baker. It's the only place in the entire city that serves a decent pastrami sandwich. Give Angelo a good talking to. He's way outta line." Angelo was a soldier, who fancied himself as a hotshot. A lesson had to come from the top, rather than from his immediate capo. "He should do the right thing and marry the daughter. He put her in the family way." Then he chuckled. "Or as the boss said, he put a bun in her oven."

Brac smiled, but Bric looked puzzled.

Jimmy was disappointed. "Okay, get outta here. And Brac, explain it to Bric."

Outside Brac said: "Angelo put a bun in the baker's daughter's oven. Gettit?"

"Yeah. Course I do. But what oven?"

Although he felt as if he had been asleep for months, he did not wake up feeling refreshed. What had probably disturbed him was the mute grumbling in his stomach. When had he last eaten? Yes, he should eat something. He had absolutely no appetite, but he should eat.

He swung his legs off the bed and sat up. A couple of flies buzzed about. His motion was strange. Parts of his body appeared to move independently and at different times and speeds and not in a coordinated way, as if he was disjointed. Even when he was still, subterranean parts of him seemed to be underway. His stomach particularly was alive. He needed to settle it.

He was gassy too. What a pong. His hands, arms, ankles and calves itched. He checked them all. They looked as if they'd been nibbled. Bed bugs? Yes, that would explain a lot.

More pesky flies seemed to appear from nowhere.

He went to his lounge, noticing that it needed a good clean. There was a film of dust on the bare sideboard. His flat was bereft of adornment. No clutter. Unsentimental. Minimalistic. Was that a cobweb in the corner of the ceiling?

The air was stale too. He would open a window.

Before reaching the refrigerator he nearly doubled-over with the writhing in his stomach. Did drugs last this long? And how long had it been? Hours? Days? Months? He had no idea.

In nearly doubling-over he pressed his hands against his torso. He was horrified to feel movement, despite the layers of his attire. What the hell. He wanted to tear off his clothes, but had to laboriously open his waistcoat and his shirt before he could lift his vest. When he did, what happened caused him to stagger backward. A cloud of flies took to the air. He fell upon the sofa and looked at where his stomach should be, to see instead a mass of squirming maggots. This trip was a never-ending nightmare. Would he ever come out of it?

All he could do was sit looking at what was once his belly. He knew the mirror would show him whole, but he wanted to will-away the illusion himself. He was so absorbed by the maggots he didn't hear his visitors arrive.

Brac looked up when one of them cleared his throat.

Jimmy and the boss stood before him. Jimmy had been the one to clear his throat and he appeared angry. He was glaring directly at him. The boss stood still but was looking about the room.

There was something not quite right with either of them.

94

Because he was transfixed by Jimmy's stare, he took in his appearance first. Jimmy had never been fat. He was too frenetic to be slowed by bodyweight. But he now appeared emaciated and his suit hung from him. Worse than his gauntness, was the left side of his face. It was ravaged. His left eye was socket black and made his other eye appear to bulge like an orb, as if it was about to pop out.

Of course Brac knew better than to ask him about it. You never asked. You were only ever told. And if the boss or Jimmy did not want to tell, then okay. You never asked.

"What are you doing here?" said Jimmy. The movement of his mouth was strange. He showed much more of his teeth than he normally did. He had always sneered, but showing more teeth exaggerated it.

Duh, thought Brac, but said: "I live here."

Jimmy's eyes dulled. Brac knew the expression. It was one of profound disappointment, often heralding some form of violence. Did he know he had not made the hit? Before he could think any further, the boss spoke.

"Nice pad," he said.

"Thanks boss," he said. But he remained wary.

Then he took in the boss's appearance. In contrast to Jimmy he had always been portly. The boss liked to eat well. But whereas Jimmy was now withered, the boss was unrecognisably bloated. Even the ring on his pinky had disappeared in a trench in his flesh.

Yet, the boss's skin looked loose, as if it had detached itself from his body. He was glistening too. Was he was sweating? In fact he was dripping and did not notice that he was standing in a puddle.

The two of them must have just come from a restaurant, because the boss especially smelt of fish. Was that a sash of kelp over his shoulder? This was so unlike him. Had he let himself go?

"We've come to take you with us."

This could be a euphemism – Brac liked the word. The boss had used it, and it made Brac sound educated when he said it. "I ain't done nothin' wrong, boss. I know–"

Jimmy piped up, his voice a rush of hostility.

"Don't you get it, you schmuck?" Brac hated being put down. "They hit us. They got me cold in the street, knocked out the boss's bodyguards–"

The boss silenced Jimmy with a weary movement of a hand.

"He's right, Brac. Nolan –" he was the organisation's consigliere – "ratted us out." Brac's reaction, caused him to add: "He got his comeuppance. Nobody likes a rat, not even those you rat to. They sliced him up." He paused. "They took me out to sea, trussed me up proper with chains and locks and lumps of metal and threw me overboard." He paused. "Worse than that was listening to that cigarillo-puffing jerk, gloating over all the changes he was going to make as the new Eastside boss."

Brac couldn't help himself and spoke out of turn for the first time in his long career. "But I got hit by lightning. That's all. It's given me some funny dreams. But I feel okay, boss. Just tired. I can still get him for you."

"Look here," said his boss and he pointed downward.

They were on a higher roof looking down upon a prone decomposing body in a Crombie at the edge of the roof below.

"They popped you in the back of the head as soon as you came out to take the shot. They took your piece and left you there to rot for the last two months."

Brac looked from one to the other, for now they were either side of him.

"We came back for you," said Jimmy, all teeth and one goggling eye.

The boss grinned and a pincer appeared at the corner of his mouth, then a small crab climbed out. The little fellow stopped at his chin to clean the periscope-stalks of his eyes with his small pincers, pulling on them and releasing them to bounce back.

"Buddies stick together," said the boss.

Return of the seaman

On board he preferred the name Chip. Nearly all ship's carpenters were nicknamed Chippy, much the same as the communications officer was often called Sparks or derivatives thereof. But Chippy sounded like a heroic pet of some treacly family television show; and Chips was a television show (cops on bikes), but also French fries in England. So he always introduced himself as Chip. "Just one of me. Chip, singular. You get chips from the chippy. And I'm neither of those."

If anyone asked after his father, he'd say that he had called him the Old Block, spinning a yarn around him being old-fashioned, fabricating stories of an Iron-Curtain nature, but really setting up the listener for the punch-line, that he, Chip, was of the old block. Yeah, that should have been *off* the old block, rather than *of* the old block, but said fast enough nobody noticed.

The train rocked from side to side, swaying his head. Being a seafarer the motion didn't bother him as much as it did the other passengers. He couldn't sleep, but tried to doze, steadying his head by lightly pressing it into the headrest wing of his seat. He couldn't sleep because his mind was too active. He probably appeared as dull and unapproachable as his fellow passengers, remote commuters travelling up to London for a day in the office or whatever. Southampton to Waterloo.

Even if they were seasoned commuters, the motion bothered them; the journey to work at this ungodly time in the morning was not a joyful experience. The joke was that the return journey was no different. Yes, the day was behind them, an evening to look forward to, but the train trip was again dead time, dulling them and accentuating their lack of energy, putting them into the closest thing to suspended animation. So a lot of them adopted this same morning aloofness and dozed their way home. Waterloo to Southampton. Woe betide a busker or beggar bother them on either of these trips: shoot the singer, execute the entertainer, blast the beggar.

But Chip was smiling inside. If he had a singer's voice, a chocolaty bass, he'd jump up and start singing *The Passenger*. And everyone simply wouldn't be able to help themselves, they would get up and dance in the aisles or swing with the music, or at least, stomp their feet, click their fingers, nod their heads and if none of these things, then they'd bloody well smile.

He was happy. He was happy because the decision had been made; the day had at long last come. Yes, he was apprehensive, but under the tremendous weight of his optimism he squashed this apprehension down.

When he'd stepped off the ship that morning, he had finally given up a life at the sea for one on terra firma. In seaman's terms he had swallowed the anchor. After more than forty-years it was truly an auspicious day, all the more so for the fact of it being the eve of his wife's birthday.

Her name was Beatty, in honour of her grandmother, someone she never knew, having died when her own mother was a toddler. All very well, except, even back then, it was such an old fashioned name. The young Beatty hated her name and from school onwards she insisted on being addressed Bea (pronounced Bee), which occasionally resulted in playground cries of being told to buzz off.

They say opposites attract and Chip and Bea were the perfect example. She was a petite, compact little woman. He was tall and thin and as a boy somewhat gangly, his arms hanging extraneously and only comfortable when they were active. She had a pretty pixie-like face: big eyes and button-nosed, so that he sometimes teased her by calling her *Tinker Bell*. He had a big face, the dominating feature being his bulbous nose, resembling that of the actor Gérard Depardieu. However, the sparkle in his mischievous eyes coupled with his wit, so successfully distracted anybody from this feature that they saw past his potato nose to a bright infectiously happy face.

But yes, he'd been mocked as a schoolboy, especially after a David Attenborough animal programme featured the proboscis monkey. He'd been called Probo for a few weeks. Luckily the name didn't stick and his humour won through.

Naturally, Chip the clown grew tired of being bubbly and had flat-times. Then his protective jovial veneer would abandon him and he'd become tender and vulnerable. Likewise, Bea wasn't always timid and accommodating; sometimes she caught him off-guard by being stubborn and feisty. But these were the exceptions to the rule that governed their relationship.

Although together, they were quite self-sufficient. She was a big reader and devoured novels and magazines. Her one failing was following some of the television soaps, which he derisively called soups: watered down leftovers with little meat. Bea took pleasure in cooking and baking, and spent epic summer days making various jams, often using the fruits of her garden labours, for the winter months and as presents for almost the entire community. Yes, she enjoyed gardening too.

For when he wasn't away at sea, Chip spent many an hour in the cellar, two rooms of which he'd fashioned for his carpentry: one as a storeroom, the other in which to work the wood. Working on ships he'd specialised in repair, rather than intricate cabinet-making. Of course his skill wasn't limited to wood. He was quite handy with metal too. Many a time he'd had to marry both as a high-seas jury rig (another seafaring term taken and given new meaning by the landlubbers) to see them through to harbour and proper repair. In a nutshell, he had to be inventive.

The two materials lent perfectly to his hobby, where he made some extra money.

Chip made medieval weaponry, but especially

crossbows.

When the opportunity presented itself he'd set up at a medieval village show or battle re-enactment as a sideshow allowing kids and adults to fire one of his replica crossbows. He had a latchet crossbow for the ladies and girls, which he'd originally made for Bea, because she couldn't cock a full-sized crossbow. Her arms and shoulders didn't have the muscle to pull the rope cocking-device whilst holding down the crossbow with one foot in the stirrup. Although the lever of the latchet crossbow made it easier to cock, she simply didn't take to it or the sport. The feather-light trigger he'd made especially for her had also taken her by surprise, firing off the first bolt before she'd been ready. He saw her failing as not having enough patience for things that called for patience. Worse than this, as far as he was concerned, she quite often got herself in a tizz before throwing in the towel. Once her confidence was broken, and to his chagrin, she gave up and refused point blank to pursue activity.

Instead Bea would make soup and bake bread to recipes of the period. So that attended these events together, she doing her thing and he doing his. They participated not to make money – they barely broke even – but for the sheer fun of it.

With more time on his hands he now hoped to increase his production. He had participated in some tournaments around the country, but he was never a serious contender.

He'd come fifth once. Much like with the medieval shows he was now present for the fun and he didn't compete. There was always the chance of making a sale or getting some orders. Although, rather than his weapons of old, competitor's of course favoured the modern crossbow: high-tech, light-weight, compound things, complex affairs with wheels and pulleys and carbon-fibre bolts. However, some competitors were also enthusiasts and, if they had a bob or two to spare, would purchase such a crossbow as an ornament.

The passengers, in the know, were up well before the train pulled into Waterloo station. They lined the aisle and confined him to his seat. Not that he was in a hurry. Let them rush off to the jobs as soon as the doors open. Rats in a race.

He idly looked outside, at the blank windows of the mean houses with their backs to the railway. He surveyed the high grimy walls; saw the sleepers, slabs of concrete, with twists of thick rust-encrusted metal fixing the black rails with their worn silver tops, embedded in long mounds of hard rusty stone. This was the worst of the city: its underbelly. The seedy areas, like dark alleyways housing the homeless in cardboard and corrugated encampments, hidden in plain-sight between the camera-flash facade of plush red-carpeted cinemas and theatre, the landmark buildings, monuments, famous place names.

The screech of the wheels and creaking of the carriages jarred any attempts at harmonious thought.

He hated city-life and could not understand why one willingly became a rat: a grey rat in a grey city. There was no racing in the village. Yes, many commuted to one of the cities, but the village was relaxed, almost sleepy. Unlike others it didn't feature on the tourist map. It wasn't a picturesque chocolate box village. Neither was it shabby. It was simply so like many others in the area as to seem ordinary. Travellers simply passed through without noticing. So it was never invaded or overrun by sightseers. Occasionally a wayward backpacker would appear, bewildered and numbed by the place, which was how the locals liked it, so that the stranger never lingered. The locals were not unfriendly. On the contrary many were excessively accommodating, even charming, certainly enough to raise the hackles of the most naive of visitors, inevitably resulting in their hasty departure.

Then they were gliding into the station, slowing, slowing and then jolting to a stop. The people in the aisle wavered forward and then backward, grabbing seatbacks and each other, the latter with an apologetic smile. Chip mused that this last jerk was done on purpose by the train driver, to wake up anyone still sleeping; a not-so-subtle slam on the brakes. He filed the idea for a possible dinner evening anecdote.

Chip waited until the last of the rats had scurried off before grabbing his sailor bag and duffle bag from the overhead rack. He slipped the rope of the former over his head and carried the other by the handles in front of his legs because of the narrowness of the aisle.

He paused for a person also grabbing a bag and glanced down at a folded national newspaper on a nearby table. A commuter had left it for someone to take. And maybe the person who had left it wasn't the one who originally bought it, for it looked particularly grubby. Recycled, like the weary grey paper with its smeared cheap ink. No doubt just handling it would leave your hands black. And it'd be indelible like a paint bomb in a rigged bag of money, evidence admissible in a court of law to the fact that you handled the newspaper. Another dinner anecdote, perhaps?

As if to underscore the depravity of the city, the headline referred to a scandal surrounding a particularly wily government minister. The Fleet Street hounds had sniffed blood and the chase was on. So far he'd out-foxed them. There was a block of smaller text near it; under the bold heading Creeper Strikes Again. He speed read the short text. The burglar-rapist known as "The Creeper" struck again last night. For a month he has been terrorising... (continued on page 4).

What a mess, he thought. Thank heavens he didn't live in the city but at the other end of the country.

Naturally, he carried a treasure-trove of outrageously salty stories of what he had seen and heard on his travels. And it was very true: city-life was the same the world over. So maybe he was being a bit harsh on his capital city.

The person in front of him moved on and Chip shuffled forward.

He gave himself up to the anonymity of the big city and became one of the expressionless people, set with tunnel-vision purpose, he so despised. From Waterloo he took the Bakerloo line up to Oxford Circus, where he changed on to the Victoria line up to King's Cross St. Pancras. From here he boarded a train to take him northwards, out of the city to Harpenden.

He'd been up since four-thirty. The slap-up English breakfast he'd had at five, which had carried him through to Waterloo, was now a torturous memory. All the chopping and changing had distracted him from buying a snack. By the time he arrived at Harpenden station it was past a quarter to eleven, which was a silly time to suffer the pangs of hunger. Lunch with Imogen and Lars could be as early twelve, so he shouldn't buy a snack.

There was not enough room in the telephone box for his bags and he left them outside, watching them between dialling and continuously afterwards.

Imogen picked up after the fourth ring.

"Hi, Im," said Chip, her name pronounced like 'him' without the aitch. "I'm here."

"Hey, Chip. Okay. He's on his way. See you soon."

He hung up and went and stood outside, resisting the urge to go to the coffee shop to get something to eat.

Chip didn't hesitate when he spotted a nearby cart selling local produce and also had a small selection of flowers. Now that he was being picked up, he didn't need to worry about carrying his two bags, in addition to a bouquet of flowers.

Some ten minutes later Chip, spotting Lars in his car, had his bags off the pavement, the flowers resting in their crinkly paper like a leg of lamb between the handles of one.

Lars pulled over and set his hazard lights flashing.

"Looking good," he said, getting out of the car to open the boot.

"You too," Chip returned. He marvelled that such a large Scandinavian could feel comfortable in such a pokey town car. Surely, he should be driving a fat four-wheel drive?

Lars, in working overalls and small run-around car, projected a very ordinary appearance, that didn't so much as hint at his wealth.

Chip handed his bags to Lars, who arranged them in the boot. He held onto the flowers, taking them to the passenger seat.

They didn't speak until they were underway.

"How are you?" asked Chip.

"Can't complain." Although the reply was a knee-jerk one, Lars certainly had nothing to complain about. As a character he wasn't as openly jolly as Chip, but he was especially satisfied where he had landed himself in life.

"And Im?"

"Also good. What about Bea?"

"Fine... Since I last spoke to her."

Lars gave him a questioning glance.

"I spoke to her yesterday," said Chip. "I called from Le Havre, but pretended I was in the Lisbon. She's expecting me to call tomorrow – it's her birthday – and be home the day after that."

Lars shook his head, his smile lopsided. "You're surprising her by turning up today."

"By the time I get there, it'll be tomorrow: her birthday."

"You should have gone straight there."

"If I'm down this end of the country, I might as well pop in, right? Anyhow, how's business?"

"So good, I'm glad you're retired. You have retired, right?"

"Yes."

"I can give you as much as you can take on."

"Sounds good."

"Bea may not think so."

"Ach, she's used to her own company."

"She's had no choice," Lars chuckled.

They drove in silence for a stretch. Lars was right. The only choice left to Bea was not to marry him. If you married a seafaring man, you couldn't expect anything else, could you?

He knew she wasn't completely comfortable on her own. The only way he could handle her worry was by being blasé. She knew this and gave herself no time to worry by keeping herself exceedingly busy. In fact she had stopped showing him any worry, so much so, that when her best school friend said she had breast cancer, she kept it from him until he came home. "I didn't want you to trouble you," she had said.

Lars slowed the car to turn it into his drive, a gravelled area encircling an island of shrubbery and a large oak, that cast a protective shadow over the house, itself large, sprawling like two semi-detached ones in one. Lars parked the car outside the closed double-garage.

"No room inside?" said Chip, unclipping his seatbelt.

"No. The good ones are in there."

Chip wasn't sure what the good ones were now. When he was last here, he'd spotted a Porsche and a Jag. But Lars knew Chip wasn't into cars and Lars would not be so vulgar as to show off. Their shared passion resided at the back of the house.

Chip left his bags in the car, but took out a gift-wrapped box and handed it to Lars.

"For you."

Lars mildly protested that a gift was unnecessary, but accepted, gruffly and yet gracefully.

Im opened the front door before they reached it.

She was dressed in working togs, similar to Lars, quite shabby. But she was the kind of woman who looked stunning no matter what she wore. She was the epitome of the Scandinavian blonde. Her dark eyes and resting expression was sulky, almost insolent, and to a stranger she appeared icy and unapproachable.

But Chip was given the welcoming smile, which appeared slightly awkward and sat uncomfortably on her face, for it didn't fit with her general demeanour. The welcome and its warmth emanated from her obvious acceptance, a disintegration of her mask, rather than the flawed expression itself. Much like Chip's humour distracted people from his nose.

"Gorgeous as ever," said Chip, handing her the flowers and holding her by the shoulders and kissing her on both cheeks, continental style.

"Oh, I am a mess," she said, stepping back to allow them in. She opened the flowers and said that they were wonderful.

Yes, Lars had every reason to be content: a beautiful wife and a beautiful home.

"Lunch will be ready in an hour," she said.

Chip rode the body blow to his aching stomach by saying: "Looking forward to it. I last ate at five."

"I'll tell cook to hurry," she said.

"You should have bought something," said Lars.

"And spoil my lunch?"

"Scotland is rubbing off on you," said Lars, implying that he was tight with his money.

"Yer bum's oot the windae."

Lars gave him a lopsided smile. Im's confusion prompted Chip to explain. "Your bum is out the window – you're talking rubbish."

The explanation didn't dispel her confusion, but she chose to dismiss further discussion. "I'll come and get you." She knew they were both dying to get down to business. "Then we can talk," she added, touching Chip's forearm and shattering her beauty with a quick smile. Almost as an afterthought, giving him a spectacular scowl, she said: "but no Scottish."

"I promise."

"I take back the Scottish bit," said Lars, who'd taken the wrapping paper off the box and was reading about the rare champagne cognac inside.

With that she went elsewhere and Lars led Chip through to the back of the house. They went through the sliding glass door on to the stone terrace and took a path around the oval pool, until they reached the expanse of lawn, which further out deteriorated to a grassy wasteland, ending some fifty metres away at a high wooden fence. Just inside this far fence there stood three straw archery target butts.

The day hadn't quite made its mind up, whether it was

going to cloud over and be grey, like early morning in the city, or loosen up and allow the sun to really shine. For the moment the sun played peek-a-boo with the continental drifts of cloud.

They followed the irregular stepping stones embedded in the lawn past some trees to the long squat building.

Lars unlocked the two locks on the heavy door. He always kept the place locked, unless it was occupied. A poster showed silhouettes of a pistol, a bottle with the letter ALC on the label and a dog. All three were crossed through with a slanted red bar each; meaning no firearms, no alcohol and no animals.

They entered a small room which, despite the desk and drawing board, wasn't quite an office, and despite the carpeted corner with easy chair, standing lamp and shelves of books, wasn't quite a study. Neither was it a den nor a sanctum. Lars had a library-cum-office in the house, complete with winged-backed chairs at an open fire and a well-stocked cocktail cabinet. Chip called it the Oval Office; though it was rectangular.

They went through the only other door, which Lars also had to unlock into the workshop, which resembled a long warehouse. The silence was eerie but welcome. Here, right and left stood half a dozen benches and vices, all manner of woodwork and metalwork tools arranged on shelves on the walls, if not hanging from boards on the walls themselves.

Beyond these benches stood a lathe, not far from a kiln for melting metal – or burning pizzas. Overhead, in the rafters, lay two ladders, sheets of metal and planks of various woods in various lengths. Two of the vices held pieces of cut wood: work in progress. Clustered in a corner, almost as a sorry afterthought, were a lawnmower, wheelbarrow and other gardening implements. Beyond all this stilled activity was a further door housing, for want of a better word, the armoury.

Lars glowed with pride as he unlocked this door.

Chip loved this room too.

A few mannequins dressed in coat-of-arms livery or even in full Knight's plate armour stood about rigidly as if on guard. Stacked or leaning, or in boxes, on shelves or benches were shields, loose swords, knives and daggers some in scabbards, hand axes, maces, military flails with spiked balls, longbows, lances, flags, peasants' clothing in drab, rough fabric, even a monk's smock, thick leather belts, ornate buckles and brooches, pockmarked target silhouettes of boars, deer, wolves and popinjays (wooden birds mounted on poles), almost everything replicas and manufactured by Lars and his team and the clothing by Im and her seamstresses.

Elsewhere, secure in rented storage units, Lars had more of the same and also his prized trebuchet.

This was all white noise to Chip, for at the end wall of the room hung the crossbows, resembling a motley squadron of model planes.

Lars too was a crossbow enthusiast, but he'd branched out into all forms of old weaponry. That said; he had been commissioned on a handful of occasions to make a futuristic-looking weapons that didn't necessarily need to work. He mostly rented his stock, but for the right price pieces could be bought. In the field of medieval weaponry Lars was a television and film advisor. He'd worked on many period films, but science fiction and fantasy ones too. He'd even done reproductions for theatre and museums. Lars was top dog in this niche and as such the envy of many. Nowadays he had so much work he was forced to sub-contract.

Chip and he went way back, to when Lars was at his level. They'd hit it off at a tournament. Whereas Chip had gone to sea, making a crossbow here and there, Lars had stayed put and made a name for himself, tailoring his work and business to that of the entertainment world. Chip sold a couple of crossbows back then, but he only started to make money, when Lars employed him to make crossbows (he'd made a shield and two daggers too) on spec.

Chip spotted the 17th century Balestrino. This all metal weapon, sometimes called an assassin's crossbow because of its toy-like size – it could easily be concealed under robes – had a screw-jack and sliding trigger block and would have been easier (like using a cork-screw) for Bea to cock. But by then, after dismissing the latchet crossbow she was adamant in her disinterest. She'd rejected the windlass – pedal-like affair – method of cocking too. Chip had to admit the last few hand-turns of such crossbows were tough going.

"Here she is," said Lars, lifting a crossbow from the wall, admiring it for a moment, before passing it to Chip.

"She's a beaut, Lars," he said, turning it this way and that, and then putting the butt to his shoulder and tipping his head to take aim. "Sits nice, too."

"Fifteenth century," said Lars. "Munitions grade. I use a goat's foot lever. Cherry-wood stock. All very basic." Chip was looking at the side plates that reinforced the socket. Unlike a hunting bow they were purely functional and plain, without etching. The steel bow and front foot-stirrup were chunky and unadorned. This was a war bow: purely functional. "We'll try her out after lunch."

Chip handed it back and Lars rehung it.

They returned to the Oval Office.

Lars pulled down a file from a shelf; opened it on the drawing board, chose the relevant separating card and flicked over to the plastic sleeve containing the construction plans. He slid out the top copy and handed it to Chip.

For a while they talked of the specifications and things to watch for when making the weapon.

"How many do you want?" said Chip.

"Ten. You know the price. I need them by the end of next month. So you've got plenty of time."

They were talking about materials when a bell sounded.

Chip smiled, for the sound reminded him of a change of watches at sea. Lars and Im had a bell (actually a child's replica Norman helmet without the nose guard) mounted on the wall near the terrace entrance.

"Food," said Lars unnecessarily.

They went back to the house, washed their hands, hovering around at the dining table, Chip recognising his flowers in a vase on the stylish sideboard, until Im came in and told them to sit as she pulled out a chair for herself.

Their part-time cook wheeled in a trolley of soup bowls and a pan of soup. This was the starter of a three course meal, an English roast, typical of a Sunday, and rather extravagant for a weekday. The certainly didn't eat like this every day and Chip knew they had gone to the trouble for him. Conversation was easy and meandering.

A shot of alcohol after such a heavy meal would have been welcome. But Lars and Chip agreed not to taste the cognac until much later, after trying out the crossbow and before Chip was to leave.

Two thirty that afternoon found them at the shooting range beyond the pool, next to the workshop and a little beyond.

The day had finally chosen to open up into a bright summer's afternoon, with next to no breeze: ideal shooting weather, if not a mite too warm.

"She's got a bit of a kick," said Chip, firing her for the

first time.

"Yeah, she tends to lift more than kick-back, don't you think?"

They spoke of her power and uninspiring chunkiness: the stock a simple block of wood. Later bows were shaped, the wood sanded smooth to be ergonomically moulded. The securing metal plates were plain, whereas later engraving and sculpturing were added.

The longbow may have the advantage of comparatively rapid fire, but the medieval crossbow was undoubtedly more a work of art.

They spent almost two hours chatting about weaponry and contracts and the general state of business, as they practised with the crossbow and other bows.

Im dropped Chip off at Harpenden station around four o'clock. As agreed, after finishing outside, Lars and he had returned to the house and tried the cognac. Lars was so impressed he insisted on them having another. He had a zero tolerance attitude to alcohol and driving and Im had agreed to take Chip to the station.

She literally dropped him off. He retrieved his bags from the boot, whilst she remained in the driver's seat, the engine idling. So he had a good ten minutes wait for his train back to the city. He was mildly, but warmly befuddled by the alcohol and as he stood on the platform, he regarded the sunshine, the trees and bushes, the sounds of nature, and yes, the graffiti and debris. All of it was wonderful, clear and bright. He was in the here and the now and life was good.

Unfortunately, the arrival of the train heralded a slow change in his attitude. The journey back to the city lulled and dulled him. He only allowed himself to doze when he was comfortably seated on the five o'clock Euston to Glasgow train, eating a purchased sandwich about half-past six. This was the long leg of his journey. After that he had almost an hour to Kilmarnock, then a fifteen minute taxi ride to his house in Springside. If all went well, he'd be home a little before midnight.

He was too tired to read and his mind too active to sleep. He let his thoughts meander. The future was uncertain, but there were vague plans. At lunch he had spoken about one.

"You're on land for good then," said Lars.

"Yes and no," he answered good-humouredly and popped a piece of beef in his mouth to give him time to enjoy their suspense. "I've booked us a Caribbean cruise."

"Good for you," said Im, cutting a roast potato. The phrase, although very English and no doubt picked up here, sounded foreign in her accent.

"When?" asked Lars.

"In just over three weeks."

Lars sipped from his glass of water, before picking up his utensils. "I assume Bea doesn't know."

Chip smiled. "No. It's a surprise."

"Birthday present?" said Lars.

"Yep."

"You and your surprises," said Im. He had already told them that he was arriving earlier than Bea expected. "I would not stand for them."

The thought of commenting on her lack of humour flashed through his mind. The British could not only laugh at anything, they could also laugh at themselves, Im was one of those typical Europeans who seemed incapable of appreciating such humour. For them black or gallows humour was worse than unfunny, it was cruel.

"Bea takes it on the chin," he said. "Do you know what she said to me, the first time I went away and I said: absence makes the heart grow fonder?"

He again used a mouthful of food, to delay his answer.

"Absence makes the fond heart wander."

"Good for her," said Lars, chuckling. Although he echoed his wife here, it sounded much more natural.

"You've got to have a laugh in this life. It's serious enough at it is."

"You know about the Creeper?" said Im.

"Yeah. I saw something in a paper this morning."

"I'm so glad Lars is here," she said.

Chip smiled and nodded.

"I am sure Bea will be pleased to have you home," she

added.

"Maybe." They were silent for a moment. "She may want to see the back of me after a few months. The longest I've been home is about four."

"I am sure it will be fine."

"Yes," said Lars. "You've each learnt to occupy yourselves alone."

The train to Glasgow went without mishap. But the one to Kilmarnock stopped in the middle of nowhere for a good twenty minutes without explanation. The usual reasons did the rounds amongst the passengers: engine problems, signal problems, a delayed train on the line, farm animals strayed onto the track or someone deciding to end it all.

Then inexplicably they started rolling again.

He almost sighed with relief when he climbed into the only taxi standing outside the station. At five past midnight there were sometimes none there and he had to call.

Once underway the taxi driver probed, and although Chip was completely weary from travelling, he pulled himself together, partly to shake himself out of his slumber, and indulged in small talk with the man. Road works, with temporary traffic lights, on the main road out of the city stopped them for far too long, with nothing far and wide. Nonetheless the chatter was welcome and helped pass the time.

Then he was standing in front of their house. By the

time he had carried his bags to the front door, the taxi was well gone and the entire road hushed and dark except for the street lighting.

He pushed his key into the lock and turned it quietly. Just as quietly he set his bags down in the carpeted hallway. He closed the door, holding back the latch to make no sound. The street light that shone through the small frosted-glass window at the top of the door was enough illumination for him to see the forms of his bags, which he carried into their lounge-diner to his left.

Only after silently closing the door onto the hallway, did he switch on the light. He took in the room for a moment, disappointingly familiar and yet refreshing as if seeing it anew. He didn't notice any changes to explain his feeling. In front of him was the cherry wood dining table surrounded by its eight matching stiff backed chairs – modern but in an antique style with curved wood armrests. Almost the entire wall opposite door, stood a number of wall units, their wood darker and richer than the dining furniture, but still with a reddish hue, burgundy. Some sections were open shelves, housing family photographs (the couple were childless); others supported closed doors on all manner of stuff; another held sliding glass doors behind which was an ornamental tea-set (an heirloom); further down, towards the back of the house, was a cocktail cabinet housing glasses and his prized whisky collection; next to this was his music system, under which were records and CDs from his youth, which he couldn't bring himself to part with. At this end of the room, looking out onto their garden, stood the television opposite the small sofa and easy chair, where, if they weren't watching something, he'd sit and listen to his music, savouring a toddy and she'd read or stitch. Small side-tables stood either end of the sofa. The local newspaper topped a pile of three or four magazines sitting on the side-table nearest him. This was the only untidiness in the room, otherwise everything was spick and span. In fact, the room smelt of furniture wax and polish and needed a desperate airing.

Chip dropped down, undid his laces and slipped off his shoes. He then turned to his bag and pulled out the bottle of champagne.

He took it down the room and was about to put it on the shelf of the kitchen hatch when the paper caught his eye. The headline was something about the Creeper. Then he thought he heard movement upstairs and he froze listening for confirmation. None came. But he decided the bottle should go into the fridge, just in case she was awake.

He moved swiftly but stealthily back to the door and opened it, leaving the light on. He turned left and entered the kitchen, going straight to the fridge. Despite opening it carefully the suction caused the appliance door to judder and the bottles and jars in the door clinked. He cursed, but quickly found a space on a shelf and slid the bottle onto it. After closing the fridge door carefully, he crept swiftly back into the lounge, where he again shut the door.

As he bent to his bag he thought he heard movement. And once more he froze to listen for a confirming creak in the house. Just as he was about to move he received his confirmation: two creaks overhead, one after the other.

He moved rapidly, placing the envelope with the cruise tickets on one of the four plate-sized lace doilies on the dining table and taking the happy birthday garland out of its cellophane wrapping. He unfolded it on the table and was pleased to see that the ends of the string would reach the books on the upper shelf of the wall unit and the light fitting above the table. On a dining table chair at the wall unit he lifted a heavier book and pushed a good length of the garland string under it. Cautiously stepping onto a doily which was like stepping upon a skateboard – such was the rich shine of the table – he reached with the other end of the garland string to the light fitting.

Was that crack the sound of somebody on the stairs?

Chip was tying the string when the door burst open and Bea stood looking at him, her eyes and mouth gaping with horror. She obviously hadn't expected anyone elevated before her and the loaded latchet crossbow she held rose reflexively. He saw her and then the bow and was about to speak when the bolt flew. At this short range the arrow would have broken through his ribcage and buried itself so deeply that only the fletching showed.

Chip instinctively lifted an arm to shield his face. In doing so, his weight shifted as his body twisted. The doily slipped under his foot and he fell backward, turning to his left. The bolt whizzed past his cheek thumping into the ceiling. He crashed onto his left side, his head almost at the far end of the table. Before Bea blocked his vision – she was hysterical, but he didn't hear her – he stared at the newspaper folded on top of the magazines on the small side table.

Kilmarnock police remain no closer to catching the Creeper, who has been terrorising the city and surroundings for the last month, in a series of burglaries and rapes of women living alone. In a statement from...

A big thank you to Tod of https://todsworkshop.com/ for his technical advice on crossbows.

Behind bars

1. Redacted

23 March

Dear Rae,

I'm not good at writing. I don't think i wrote nothing since school. I hated grammar and Mr. Green's smile. He was like a cat, you know, full of himself. But he was a weakling. Runner been green, we called him. I thought, if i could get him in an alley, i'd cut the smile off of his face. He asked me once, if the cat had me tongue. Well, i should of cut his tongue out an fed it to the alley cats. But yeah, maybe i should of paid more attenshen in school. Dont expect sentimental stuff, Rae, You know me. ▪▪▪ ▪▪▪ ▮ ▪▪▪ ▪▪▪ God, you were the best looking girl in court. All the others were vegetables or frutes. You know, prunes, dried up an all and cabbachis and bloody potatos. Ponces wearing stupid wigs on there stupid heads. I mean, what sentry we in. All serious an important like. Lots of Mr. Greens. Fuckin runner beens. Even the gards eyes were on storks. 8 years is not so bad. 8 years detained at her majestys pleasure. Poncy way of saying locking you up. It'll fly by. Maybe i get out early wiv ~~good behaveior~~ being good or somethink. I cant beleave i have wrote a half a page allready.

It must be a record or somethink. I never wrote so much in me life. I got time now. Supose. I tell you what happened when they take me down. Bastards could of let me hug you and Mum. I went into a holding cell and had to wait. I had to wait in a lot of places. Oh yeah. They said i should watch what i write. And what you write. Nothink about escape an all. ██ ██ That sort of think. But also anythink upsetting or angry. You know. Threts an all. Wynn saw me and said he would apeel and he would pass messages. Did he tell you not to worry, like what i said. Then i get handcuffed and taken to a van. This van has compartments, like toilets. But theres no loo in this van. Thats a joke isnt it. If i'm not locked up, i'm handcuffed to a uniform. An you know what. We drive for ages, stopping of to let other prisoners out. Its like that Lanzarotti holiday, when that bus drops all those people of at there hotels and you wait ages to get to yours. some of these blokes know each other and i hear them chatting. They've been in court for a hearing or somethink. They call these compartments swet boxes and there not wrong. I was in that van for hours. No clock an no fucking loo. Then we stop and i am cuffed again. Then the docs see me and check me out. An theres these forms to fill out. They call them compax. Dont know why. And i am photographed and i get an identity card and prison number. They let me make a call. Two minutes max. i phoned you, but you weren't in. So i phoned mum and didn't know what to say.

Then i was given an insider to show me the ropes. Then i meet the wing staff and get a cell. Its a two men one. Two beds. Not bunks. My cellmate is this old man. That first night i thought he might croak on me. Yea, he's that old. I forgot. They gave me 3 pear socks, 3 pants, 3 t-shirts an 2 jogging trousers. But everyone has there own cloths here. When you come you can bring some of my gear. During my first week i got what was called induction. Lechures and presentions from medical team, a preest, drug team, teachers team, probation team an gym instructer. All blah blah. Rules and regulayshons. Then i have to work or take education. I guess that's it for now. me hands ~~acki~~ hurting from holding the pen so long. The most i have ever wrote in me life. Come soon. That sounds noughty. You know nooky. No chance of that. Take care, Paul.

2 April

Dear Paul,

I can't match your letter. Nothing has happened. Your missed. But we are getting on with life and all. I haven't seen your Mum. You know she didn't like me. I called, but she was offish. You know what I meen? She thought I was abad inflence. With what happened maybe I was. She didn't like that I wore that sexy dress in court. But I knew it was your favourite. Did you notice I had me hair done? Platnum in the blond. Heavenly highlights, it's called. And that pearly nail varnish you like. Your mum didn't like it.

I will have to see her to get your stuff. I'll tell her I dressed up for you. I will come in a couple of weeks. To bad your dad doesn't want to see you. I got on good with him. Nothing more to say. Love, Rae.

10 April

Dear Rae,

It was grate seeing you. The other guys ███ ███ ███ eyes popped out. You were good for my eyes to. I wanted to eat you up. No touching, what a bummer. Thanks for the gear. Gives me a bit of style. Someone wants to buy or trade my nike tee-shirt. I might sell it. You were a bit cool, ██ ██ ██ ██ ██ ██ ██ ██ ██ ██ ██ ██ ██ ██ ██ ██ ██ I have asked around. The guys say strip searches are ██ normal. I know you were imbaraced. ██ ██ ██ ██ ██ ██ ██ ██ ██ Maybe they wont do it next time. They strip search me when i got here and i had to neel in a BOSS chair ██ ██ ██ ██ ██ ██ ██ ██ ██ ██ ██ ██ I have joined acreative writing corse. The teacher says i should walk befor running. He is going to help me with that grammar stuff. Hes ██ as ponsy as runner been. ██ ██ ██ ██ ██ ██ I have to work to. I try plumbing. You got to sign up for 4 weeks. Then stick with it or try somethink else. Mum's money is not enough for siggies and luxuries. My acount is nearly always zero here. My bastard old man wont give me a penny. Maybe you could talk to him. He liked you cause he probly fancied you for hisself. I have to trade stuff. Good that they give me pen an paper and envalope and stamp for letter writing. Its only once a week, but enuff for me. I trade some of it. some guys write every day. but there folks give them stationary an all. Everythink here is done with a form. They have a paper for everythink. I woodnt be surprised if theres one for taking a shit. Ha. Ha. I didn't tell you about Derek. He's my sellmate. He's older than me. Maybe dad's age. He's in for armed robbery. ICI, you know, Chemical place. A security gard was shot by one of the gang and died. Derek was the safe cracker an says he didn't load his gun. The law didn't believe him. Hes near the end of his sentence. ███████████ ███████████████████████████████████ He's got a tv. But you can't get disent channels. We have a curtain in front of the loo. That's as far as privacy goes. Doesn't stop the stink. An he does some ripe ones. We get locked in at 6pm and wake up is at 8am. Breakfast is in the sell. We get a pack of coffee an tea and breakfast an take it back to the sell and get locked in again. A couple of the guys have an eye on me. █ ██████████████████████████████████████ ████████████████████ I don't know why. ███ ████████ I'll show them. I can take care of myself. I don't need no one. ████████████ Maybe i can buy them off with a tee shirt. Cant be ██ ████████ ██████ ████████ ███ ███ ██ soft. █████████ You know i can take care of meself. Paul.

25 April

Dear Paul,

Thanks for your newsy letter. I had to look up BOSS chair. Body orifice security scanner. It looked like a wooden throne. I hope they didn't hurt my soldier. Derek sounds like a good person. Ha. I mean a good person for a knacky. I see your having a tough time. But your tough. I am not so tough. The train and long country bus journey were bad enough. But the strip search put me right off. There was only one officer who was nice to me. I think his name was Rodrigez. Do you know him? Don't worry, I will see you in two weeks. Nothing much to say. I haven't spoke to your mum. Your dad was funny on the phone. He new I was calling for you. And told me to tell you that you disappoint him. I didn't want to tell you like this, but I have got to write something and I know you want to know. See you soon. Love Rae.

26 May

Dear Paul,

They told me you were in soildary for fighting and couldn't have visits. What happened? They wouldn't tell me. Nothing to say, ██████████████████ They said you were in the infirmary first. Did they get you? Or you get them? What's it all about? Were you badly hurt? I suppose I shoud say what I've been doing. I went to Flashes with the girls on Saturday. ████████████████ I haven't been out proper since you went in. We had some drinks and laughs and dancing. Debbie sent the boys packing. ████████████████ Maybe you can call me as soon as your out of solidary. Love Rae.

15 June

Dear Rae,

Grate to here your voice. I am looking forward to seeing you. My P.O. – personal officer – said I should keep me head really low. Wynn said such ~~alterea~~ incidents did not reflect good on my character. He said he'd do his best. But like my P.O. said, if I got into serious trouble, you know GBH or somethink, then I wouldn't be getting out any time soon and my sentence could be extended. Bastards. It's so fucking unfair. But like what I said, someone here has got me pegged. I just don't know who is behind it. Or why. They found a radio under me pillow and said i stole it. I was set-up. Nicking adds to your sentence. I don't know nobody here who would have a grudje gainst me.

I don't know Rodrigez. Bloody daegos invading our country. I ask around and guys say hes on the level.

Rae, you should ██████ not ████████ go out. I'm just ████████ protecting my property. ██████████ ████████

Have you noticed my english has got better. It's the creative writing teacher. See you soon. Paul.

13 July

Dear Paul,

I am not sure I can come again for a while. I told you I wasn't stripped██████████████████ No one ██ was nice to me. Let me have a break for a while. Yes, your English is getting better over these months. By the time your out you will be writing like Shakespear. One thing annoys me about your letters. You never sign with love, like what I do. You never said it when we was together. I said it all the time and you said ditto or you too. I know its you being tough. But I don't show your letters to nobody. Lets phone. Love, Rae.

27 July

Dear Rae,

Our calls are always kind of awkward because there are guys in the line behind me. And ████████████ I can't be a wimp.

Being here is a drag and you have to watch your back all the time. No internet, only a couple of chanels on the tv. Derek says I should get books from the libry. Derek, lucky bastard, is having his first ROTL. It means release on temprorary license. He gets out for the day. Part of the programme for getting back in ~~society~~ soceity. I can █ understand why you won't visit. ███████████ I hate this place and ████ you all the more. ██████ ██████████ Now you know. Paul.

14 August

Dear Paul,

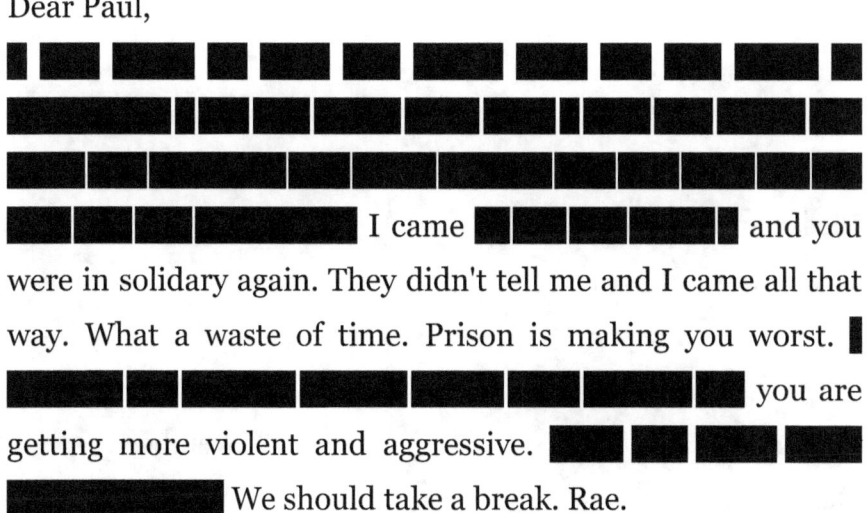

I came ██████████ and you were in solidary again. They didn't tell me and I came all that way. What a waste of time. Prison is making you worst. █ ██████████████████████████ you are getting more violent and aggressive. ████ ████ ████ ████ ██████████ We should take a break. Rae.

28 September

Dear Rae,

Why wont you take my calls? I was in isolation, ████████

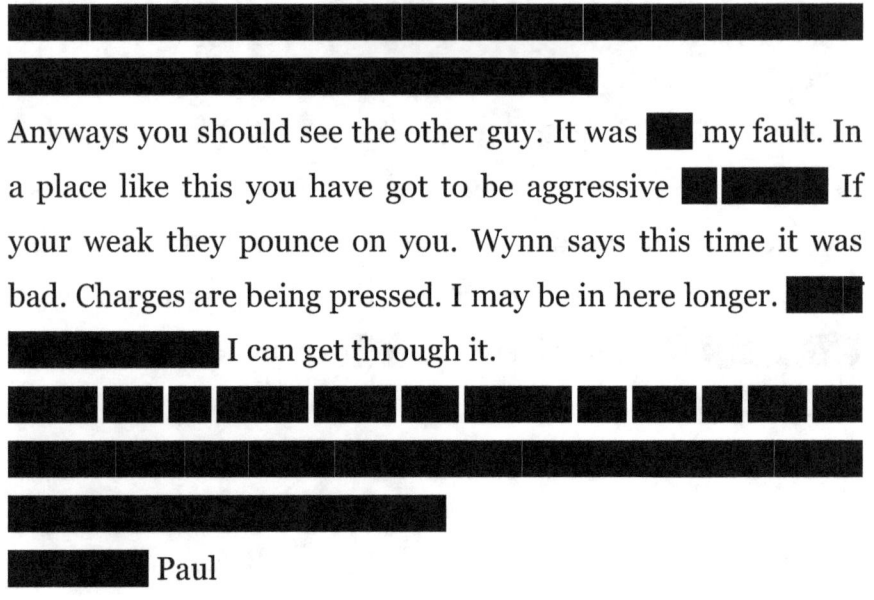

Anyways you should see the other guy. It was ▮ my fault. In a place like this you have got to be aggressive ▮▮▮ If your weak they pounce on you. Wynn says this time it was bad. Charges are being pressed. I may be in here longer. ▮▮ ▮▮▮ I can get through it.

▮▮▮▮▮▮▮▮▮▮▮▮

▮▮▮▮▮▮▮▮▮▮

▮▮▮▮▮

▮▮ Paul

17 October

Dear Rae,

Please anser.

Love, Paul

10 November

Dear Paul,

This is my last letter. Wynn says you'll be in for about ten years with good behave-your. I can't wait that long. You've got yourself to blame. Fighting. Playing the hard man. Thats what got you in there in the first place. I still don't know why you always carried that knife. You were lucky he had one to.

Otherwise they would have locked you up for longer. Rae.

20 December

Dear Rae,

I haven't given up. You weren't in court. So maybe you don't know they gave me 5 more years. ████████████████████ ██ ██ ██████████Fucking bastards. ████████████████████████ ██ Like I said. ██████████████ my letters ████ turned you against me. ██████████████████ We must talk. Please come back. Please reply. Call. Anythink. ██████████████ Merry Christmas, Paul.

5 January

Dear Rae,

Please reply. I beleave you didn't read what I wrote. Bring my letters to me and I'll tell you what got blacked out. Please Rae, come here. I can explain. Please write.

I need money for my account too. But its not important.

Please reply. I still need you. Love Paul.

17 January

Dear Mrs. Mills,

Please pass the enclosed letter to your daughter, Rae.

My last letter was returned: "not known at this address."

Rae, I work in the library and have read a whole book. It was called "The old man and the sea." It's a classic. I have been collecting IEPs – incentives and earned priveleges. My P.O. said I am becoming a model prisoner. With good behaviours I could be out in 8 years. That's not long.

Love, Paul.

10 February

Dear Paul,

Rae has moved abroad. She has married and doesn't want to see you. There are too many Mrs. Rodriguez for you to find. I suggest you leave her and us alone.

Yours sincerely,

Mrs. Mills.

2. Unredacted

23 March

Dear Rae,

I'm not good at writing. I don't think i wrote nothing since school. I hated grammar and Mr. Green's smile. He was like a cat, you know, full of himself. But he was a weakling. Runner been green, we called him. I thought, if i could get him in an alley, i'd cut the smile off of his face. He asked me once, if the cat had me tongue. Well, i should of cut his tongue out an fed it to the alley cats. But yeah, maybe i should of paid more attenshen in school. Dont expect sentimental stuff, Rae, You know me. Just know i need you. God, you were the best looking girl in court. All the others were vegetables or frutes. You know, prunes, dried up an all and cabbachis and bloody potatos. Ponces wearing stupid wigs on there stupid heads. I mean, what sentry we in. All serious an important like. Lots of Mr. Greens. Fuckin runner beens. Even the gards eyes were on storks. 8 years is not so bad. 8 years detained at her majestys pleasure. Poncy way of saying locking you up. It'll fly by. Maybe i get out early wiv ~~good behaveior~~ being good or somethink. I cant beleave i have wrote a half a page allready. It must be a record or somethink. I never wrote so much in me life. I got time now. Supose. I tell you what happened when they take me down. Bastards could of let me hug you and Mum. I went into a holding cell and had to wait. I had to wait in a lot of places. Oh yeah. They said i should watch what i write. And what you write. Nothink about escape an all. You know, putting a hacksaw blade in a cake or sanwich. That sort of think. But also anythink upsetting or angry. You know. Threts an all. Wynn saw me and said he would apeel and he

137

would pass messages. Did he tell you not to worry, like what i said. Then i get handcuffed and taken to a van. This van has compartments, like toilets. But theres no loo in this van. Thats a joke isnt it. If i'm not locked up, i'm handcuffed to a uniform. An you know what. We drive for ages, stopping of to let other prisoners out. Its like that Lanzarotti holiday, when that bus drops all those people of at there hotels and you wait ages to get to yours. some of these blokes know each other and i hear them chatting. They've been in court for a hearing or somethink. They call these compartments swet boxes and there not wrong. I was in that van for hours. No clock an no fucking loo. Then we stop and i am cuffed again. Then the docs see me and check me out. An theres these forms to fill out. They call them compax. Dont know why. And i am photographed and i get an identity card and prison number. They let me make a call. Two minutes max. i phoned you, but you weren't in. So i phoned mum and didn't know what to say. Then i was given an insider to show me the ropes. Then i meet the wing staff and get a cell. Its a two men one. Two beds. Not bunks. My cellmate is this old man. That first night i thought he might croak on me. Yea, he's that old. I forgot. They gave me 3 pear socks, 3 pants, 3 t-shirts an 2 jogging trousers. But everyone has there own cloths here. When you come you can bring some of my gear. During my first week i got what was called induction. Lechures and presentations from medical team, a preest, drug team, teachers team, probation team an gym instructer. All blah blah. Rules and regulayshons. Then i have to work or take education. I guess that's it for now. me hands ~~acki~~ hurting from holding the pen so long. The most i have ever wrote in me life. Come soon. That sounds noughty. You know nooky. No chance of that. Take care, Paul.

2 April

Dear Paul,

I can't match your letter. Nothing has happened. Your missed. But we are getting on with life and all. I haven't seen your Mum. You know she didn't like me. I called, but she was offish. You know what I meen? She thought I was abad inflence. With what happened maybe I was. She didn't like that I wore that sexy dress in court. But I knew it was your favourite. Did you notice I had me hair done? Platnum in the blond. Heavenly highlights, it's called. And that pearly nail varnish you like. Your mum didn't like it.

I will have to see her to get your stuff. I'll tell her I dressed up for you. I will come in a couple of weeks. To bad your dad doesn't want to see you. I got on good with him. Nothing more to say. Love, Rae.

10 April

Dear Rae,

It was grate seeing you. The other guys and the screws eyes popped out. You were good for my eyes to. I wanted to eat you up. No touching, what a bummer. Thanks for the gear. Gives me a bit of style. Someone wants to buy or trade my nike tee-shirt. I might sell it. You were a bit cool, but you said the screws gave you a hard time. But this place does that to you. Dehumanizes. Dehumanises. I have asked around. The guys say strip searches are not normal. I know you were imbaraced. I think some of the women screws are lesbions. Maybe they wont do it next time. They strip search me when i got here and i had to neel in a BOSS chair so then check my orafices. Bastards enjoy humil making fun of you. I have joined acreative writing corse. The teacher says i should walk befor running. He is going to help me with that grammar stuff. Hes not as ponsy as runner been. See. I'm going to better meself. I have to work to. I try plumbing. You got to sign up for 4 weeks. Then stick with it or try somethink else. Mum's money is not enough for siggies and luxuries. My acount is nearly always zero here. My bastard old man wont give me a penny. Maybe you could talk to him. He liked you cause he probly fancied you for hisself. I have to trade stuff. Good that they give me pen an paper and envalope and stamp for letter writing. Its only once a week, but enuff for me. I trade some of it. some guys write every day. but there folks give them stationary an all. Everythink here is done with a form. They have a paper for everythink. I woodnt be surprised if theres one for taking a shit. Ha. Ha. I didn't tell you about Derek. He's my sellmate. He's older than me. Maybe dad's age. He's in for armed robbery. ICI, you know, Chemical place. A security gard was shot by one of the gang and died. Derek was the safe cracker an says he didn't load his gun. The law didn't believe him. Hes near the end of his sentence. He said if i keep me head down, i could get out as early as in 5 years. He's got a tv. But you can't get disent channels. We have a curtain in front of the loo. That's as far as privacy goes. Doesn't stop the stink. An he does some ripe ones. We get locked in at 6pm and wake up is at 8am. Breakfast is in the sell. We get a pack of coffee an tea and breakfast an take it back to the sell and get locked in again. A couple of the guys have an eye on me. I think somethink might happen. But i don't want no bovver. But i think they are out to get me. I don't know why. If they come at me I'll show them. I can take care of myself. I don't need no one. Only you, corse. Maybe i can buy them off with a tee shirt. Cant be to generous. Otherwise everyone will think i'm soft. Don't worry. You know i can take care of meself. Paul.

25 April

Dear Paul,

Thanks for your newsy letter. I had to look up BOSS chair. Body orifice security scanner. It looked like a wooden throne. I hope they didn't hurt my soldier. Derek sounds like a good person. Ha. I mean a good person for a knacky. I see your having a tough time. But your tough. I am not so tough. The train and long country bus journey were bad enough. But the strip search put me right off. There was only one officer who was nice to me. I think his name was Rodrigez. Do you know him? Don't worry, I will see you in two weeks. Nothing much to say. I haven't spoke to your mum. Your dad was funny on the phone. He new I was calling for you. And told me to tell you that you disappoint him. I didn't want to tell you like this, but I have got to write something and I know you want to know. See you soon. Love Rae.

26 May

Dear Paul,

They told me you were in soildary for fighting and couldn't have visits. What happened? They wouldn't tell me. Nothing to say, except that I worry about you. They said you were in the infirmary first. Did they get you? Or you get them? What's it all about? Were you badly hurt? I suppose I shoud say what I've been doing. I went to Flashes with the girls on Saturday. Nothing happened. I haven't been out proper since you went in. We had some drinks and laughs and dancing. Debbie sent the boys packing. She knows I'm with you. Maybe you can call me as soon as your out of solidary. Love Rae.

15 June

Dear Rae,

Grate to here your voice. I am looking forward to seeing you. My P.O. – personal officer – said I should keep me head really low. Wynn said such ~~alterca~~ incidents did not reflect good on my character. He said he'd do his best. But like my P.O. said, if I got into serious trouble, you know GBH or somethink, then I wouldn't be getting out any time soon and my sentence could be extended. Bastards. It's so fucking unfair. But like what I said, someone here has got me pegged. I just don't know who is behind it. Or why. They found a radio under me pillow and said i stole it. I was set-up. Nicking adds to your sentence. I don't know nobody here who would have a grudje gainst me.

I don't know Rodrigez. Bloody daegos invading our country. I ask around and guys say hes on the level.

Rae, you should relax. I'm not sure you should go out. I'm just glad Debbie is protecting my property. But you got to protect yourself to.

Have you noticed my english has got better. It's the creative writing teacher. See you soon. Paul.

13 July

Dear Paul,

143

I am not sure I can come again for a while. I told you I wasn't stripped, but that was because of Rodrigez. No one else was nice to me. Let me have a break for a while. Yes, your English is getting better over these months. By the time your out you will be writing like Shakespear. One thing annoys me about your letters. You never sign with love, like what I do. You never said it when we was together. I said it all the time and you said ditto or you too. I know its you being tough. But I don't show your letters to nobody. Lets phone. Love, Rae.

27 July

Dear Rae,

Our calls are always kind of awkward because there are guys in the line behind me. And they can here. So I can't be a wimp. I really need you to visit. You are the only thing that keeps me going. Stand by your man. I got that orfall song in me head. Being here is a drag and you have to watch your back all the time. No internet, only a couple of chanels on the tv. Derek says I should get books from the libry. Derek, lucky bastard, is having his first ROTL. It means release on temprorary license. He gets out for the day. Part of the programme for getting back in ~~society~~ soceity. I can't understand why you won't visit. Please visit. I hate this place and love you all the more. There I have said it. Now you know. Paul.

144

14 August

Dear Paul,

I was upset by your last letter. Why are you being so aggressive? I bet you wrote need after I hate this place. The word was sensored. You know blacked out. You can't say you love me. Mr. Machoman. I came to ask you about it and you were in solidary again. They didn't tell me and I came all that way. What a waste of time. Prison is making you worst. I thought the creative writing would have helped. But you are getting more violent and aggressive. Your last letter really really upset me. We should take a break. Rae.

28 September

Dear Rae,

Why wont you take my calls? I was in isolation, but I was out when you came. They didn't call me. now they say i must have mist the call on the tannoy. Lying bastards.

Anyways you should see the other guy. It was not my fault. In a place like this you have got to be aggressive to survive. If your weak they pounce on you. Wynn says this time it was bad. Charges are being pressed. I may be in here longer. But if you stick by me I can get through it.

Derek was on ROTL when you visited. He said he saw you outside with that screw Rodriguez. If your fucking him, I'll kill you both. That'll be blacked out.

I love you. Paul

17 October

Dear Rae,

Please anser.

Love, Paul

10 November

Dear Paul,

This is my last letter. Wynn says you'll be in for about ten years with good behave-your. I can't wait that long. You've got yourself to blame. Fighting. Playing the hard man. Thats what got you in there in the first place. I still don't know why you always carried that knife. You were lucky he had one to. Otherwise they would have locked you up for longer. Rae.

20 December

Dear Rae,

I haven't given up. You weren't in court. So maybe you don't know they gave me 5 more years. And you know whose been bribing the guys in here to get me? Rodriguez. Yeah, your favourite guard. I wouldn't be surprised if he has others helping him. Fucking bastards. I think he's left and hey presto I haven't had no more bother. Proof it was him all along. Like I said. He was blacking out my letters and turned you against me Course I got no proof. We must talk. Please come back. Please reply. Call. Anythink. I need you. Love Merry Christmas, Paul.

5 January

Dear Rae,

Please reply. I beleave you didn't read what I wrote. Bring my letters to me and I'll tell you what got blacked out. Please Rae, come here. I can explain. Please write.

I need money for my account too. But its not important.

Please reply. I still need you. Love Paul.

A vanity of existence (Ark 109)

As Lub climbed the steps of the auditorium, he was so resolved to tell her today he didn't register the pull of his inhibitor on his legs. Nor did he notice the noise his soles made, or those of his classmates behind and in front of him, as they tore them from the floor stripe. The thought of approaching his educator consumed the boy so much as to shove his attentiveness to the back of his mind, almost turning him into an automaton. Over and over he pictured his action in his mind. For he had to tell her before any of his classmates did so and rendered his declaration meaningless.

Lub turned and walked to his place, careful not to snag his inhibitor on the flipped seating. He guided his electronic slate with little nudges above the continuous desktop, careful to keep it within his grasp; some of his more mischievous classmates were apt to strike another's slate away, sending it spinning to the ceiling or a corner, leaving the owner with no option other than to propel themselves after it. Many a time in the past, an educator would enter a room in utter chaos, with slates and children all over the place.

He stopped and secured his slate on the desktop, took off his gloves – you could not operate a slate in gloves – adhering them to his jumpsuit at his waist. He then pushed down his seat, feeling the vague roughness on his fingertips.

He sat, adjusting his position, as always irritated that whenever he sat he was never immediately comfortable. He always had to tear himself off the seat and reposition his buttocks. Once he had chosen not to get comfortable and after leaning onto the backrest, his shoulders adhering higher than normal, he had difficultly leaning forward. Naturally, because of the noise, he had timed his movement to coincide with a pause in the lecture, as everyone did, like the clearing throats during a physical performance scene change.

Everyone hated the inhibitors, even though they were a necessary evil. The only time they were a joy was in the gym, which they coined the sticky room. Indeed, the inhibitors were colloquially known as sticky suits. Covered in a modern derivative of something known as Velcro to the Earthers, the suits helped to slow muscle deterioration. (Embedded pulse-stimulation was not enough.) The ship was strategically covered in strips of its complement and inhibited movement, without making it impossible. Lub and company now wore adult-strength sticky suits.

When they first moved up to full strength, Dox and Weiz took special delight in picking on the puny kids by pushing them against the wall. If the length of their back was stuck, they could remain there until someone helped peel them off. Many a time one of them was penalised for being late to class.

Disapproved races in doubles involved propelling

themselves down corridors touching the ship with their sticky-gloved hands as fleetingly as possible. Occasionally, the boys especially – but not exclusively – had racing fights, in which shoving and pushing were allowed. They refined the ability during free time in the sticky room by playing tag, free-floating away from the catchers.

From the end of year one, they had been encouraged to crawl to rewards such as sweets and toys. Later they'd been assisted in mastering the art of erect walking. Many resisted. They couldn't understand why they had to endure such a cumbersome mode of motion when you could swim and propel yourself in any direction. Bland explanations of the gravitational pull of a home almost a decade away meant very little to them.

Like his classmates, give or take a couple of days, Lub was ten years old. They made up the last batch (youngest possible considering the timing of their arrival). Twenty year olds made up the next earlier batch. Then there were the thirty-year olds and the forty-year olds. These four batches made up the majority of the passengers. There were however a smattering of NBs (natural borns), more often called IBs for in-betweeners, because age-wise they did not fit in any batch. Just as NBs were rare, so too then were parents. Artificial family units existed for those thirty- and forty-year olds that wanted to be part of a family. This meant that families comprised up to ten persons (considered to be the optimal number), often with more than two leading adults.

Dox and Weiz were in a rather authoritarian unit with three adults, two law enforcers and a director – someone who, as an Earther, would have been a lawyer or judge, but also a mayor. Lub thought that was why the boys always had frustration to burn off.

Lub's own unit of six was led by a biologist and a farmer.

Of course the measurement of age in years had its roots in the history of the Earth dwellers, Earthers. The idea of hours had been retained, which, bound with the human cycle of eight-hour blocks of sleep, work and recreation had led to the 24-hour day. However, months and years had been redefined, the first being 30 days and the second being 360 days. In terrestrial terms these children were marginally younger than nine Earth-measured years (EMYs pronounced "emmies") of age.

The recommendation was to adapt the measurement of time to the natural cycles of their home, when they arrived.

The adults were trained in all manner of basic trades, many with more than one specialisation. There were tailors, cobblers, chemists, botanists, mechanics, medics, educators, etc. But to utilise the planet's resources many were versed in ancient posts: stonemasons, carpenters, blacksmiths and such.

Few knew the exact total number of frozen eggs and

sperm, but they were said to run into the millions.

As usual the children were all in their places and waiting, some more unruly than others, but waiting nonetheless. When she entered the room, even the animated ones settled. An expectant hush descended upon the auditorium.

She walked straight-backed and brisk to stand behind her desk and look them over. Satisfied that all were present, she greeted them.

"Good morning, class."

"Good morning, Educator Croo," they chorused back. Unlike some of the other educators, she insisted on formality, explaining during their very first week of schooling at two years old, that she regarded it as respectful. The Creative educator, Nardo, wasn't like that at all. He was fun and eccentric and a little wild.

Irrespective of address, all educators were beloved.

She scanned them again, assessing their disposition and wellbeing, confirming their attentiveness.

"Before we continue with our history of AI, I want to speak of the rumours that have been circulating."

Lub wasn't expecting this and his intended action was forgotten for the moment.

"It's true that we are nearing our destination. I can tell you that the planet is habitable with sufficient gravity and a suitable atmosphere. Primitive life already exists in plant and animal form." She paused. "Questions?"

She tapped her slate to connect with their slates.

The children used their slates to send messages to her, which she received and cherry-picked. Lub was tempted to carry out his intended declaration in writing there and then, but decided against it and wrote nothing.

The Educator smiled. "I'll begin by answering yours first, Erse." She looked at the boy before talking to the auditorium. "He asks whether life on the planet is dangerous. The honest answer is that we don't know. Personally, I should think that, similar to Earth, plants and animals alike could pose a danger. Considering the fact that we have discovered no evidence of civilisation, I think it's safe to say that you will be the intelligently superior beings."

She looked at a first row girl, who stiffened, but smiled uncertainly.

"Pru asks whether remaining on the ship and continuing the journey is an option. I think you all know the answer to this question, given what you have been taught about travel.

"To transcribe huge distances over long periods at speed the only way to transport humans is as frozen sperm and eggs. This circumvents nourishment problems such as food, water, air and even physical space."

She looked at Pru again. And smiled as she said: "I know your question is emotional rather than logical, Pru. But

153

travelling onward is not possible."

The Educator's various subtle expressions said that she was weighing up the pros and cons of answering further questions.

"I'll answer one more," she said. "Unge asks a very important question. She asks whether younger IBs will have a problem with the planet's gravity. Unfortunately the answer is yes. For some of them the effect on their organs will be crippling and life-threatening. Their parents were warned and advised against natural conception. We are doing all we can with electro-stimulation, exercise and medicine."

Lub watched her scan the rows. Could she tell he had something on his mind?

"We'll leave it at that for now. Next week we will be commencing an orientation course to prepare you physically and mentally for the planet and disembarkation."

She tapped her slate, connecting it with the huge screen behind her.

"Let's recap our last lesson. We started by discussing the very beginning of AI in the nineteen-fifties emmy. Back then, Earthers approached the subject by trying to find ways to build systems that could do what they themselves could do. This was termed strong AI. Earthers quickly came to the conclusion that the problem was too big to solve and instead chose to tackle simpler, feasibly-solvable problems, which was called weak AI. Around nineteen-eighty another branch of AI grew: this was not simply to mimic Earthers, but to develop the ability to learn. Deep-learning using layered neural networks emerged around two thousand emmies. Can anyone explain to me supervised and unsupervised learning?"

Lub knew a question was due about now. Educator Croo had to check they were listening, even if it was a recap. She always threw the question out as if asking for a volunteer, but then chose one of them herself.

"Fuge, can you explain?"

The boy stiffened. "Supervised learning was when an observer reviewed the outcome of an AI activity and adjusted it to make it more accurate."

"Correct," she said. "The calibration was usually carried out by an Earther, who adjusted input constants or weightings. Unsupervised learning was when the multi-layered system of algorithms was able to do this itself through, amongst other things, back-propagation: using the correct result and reversing the process making adjustments accordingly.

"You will recall that such algorithms were used in self-driving vehicles and also health analysis. Interpreting all manner of machine scans was a trivial exercise for AI and eliminated the need for medical specialists. Predictions for certain diseases or ailments in later life, such as the likelihood of someone developing dementia were made with expert accuracy. AI came to the same conclusions as any panel of

Earther experts. The difference was that these experts could explain how they came to their diagnosis; AI could not. No Earther could fathom their reasoning and AI couldn't retrace the complexity of code and contributions to explain itself. In this respect AI was already a black box. This was merely the beginning of AI exceeding human intelligence."

She paused.

Many of the children shifted position or fidgeted for a moment.

"Today we will talk about the relationship between Earthers, AI and more."

She paused again.

"Neural-networks inspired by the animal visual cortex using memory cells – remember input and output gates with information subject to a forget gate – and applying fuzzy-logic to mimic Earthers behaviour exacerbated a deep-seated mistrust of AI. Fuzzy logic replaced the chemical ingredient that influenced emotion in the organic brain, which is necessary for creativity and invention. With these building-blocks AI surpassed human comprehension and moved into the realms of artificial super intelligence or ASI. Unlike AI, ASI was more pro-active than reactive.

"By the time of ASI, Earthers reliance upon machines was absolute." Croo listed everyday examples, especially in the service industry, such as catering and cleaning, before delving into the realms of education and gaming to occupy the majority of the populace and give them an appropriate and necessary sense of worth.

She went on to outline team games and sport, social encouragement through drink and drugs – both monitored for appropriate moderation. "All aspects of society were infiltrated and optimised for the well-being of Earthers. Mental and physical deficiencies were alerted and recommendations were made for improvement. Even authors lost out to ASI stories."

Educator Croo then threw out the question of whether anyone could suggest a job that required natural humans. This was one of her catch-all questions and a rare time when she didn't pick volunteers.

No one had an answer and she admitted that there were very few. Then she suggested jobs that required human comfort or intimate connection; the personal touch required in palliative care was a good example.

"ASI was benign and answerable to itself and – because Earthers were easy to read – incorruptible. Criminal Earthers tried to manipulate ASI, but their motivation was assessed and seen to be founded in greed. Through learning and self-improvement ASI freed itself from Earthers' influence. ASI was resistant to abuse or manipulation. No Earther was capable of intellectually challenging ASI on its own level.

"Can anyone tell me when a robot could become corrupt?"

"Welt?"

Welt shook her head.

"Sel?"

Sel shrugged.

"Yes, it's a difficult question," Educator Croo said. "An accident causing physical damage could create a glitch in the code that could leap the bounds of its own coding. Then, a robot could lose its moral imperative and go rogue. Such incidents were rare and immediately put down.

"Despite this, even if Earthers didn't fear ASI and robots, many feared their own irrelevance."

Lub's attention waned and he knew to look down at his slate. Educator Croo always judged the class as a whole and when she saw their eyes glaze over and other signs she'd ask a question or introduced active participation.

His attention waned because thoughts of his action at the end of class had begun to play in his mind again. So he only half-listened.

"I will digress for a moment and talk about this fear, which you may think incomprehensible. Earthers were faced with a problem based on anthropomorphism. Can anyone tell me what this means? Lagen?"

The boy shook his head.

Lub looked up, annoyed with himself for not paying attention, quickly using his slate to recall the question.

"Yout?"

"It's, er–" he cleared his throat, "like believing things are human."

"Correct. It's attributing human processes or thinking to non-humans. It's a form of empathy. Earthers were apt to do this to explain animal behaviour, for instance." She paused. "The trouble with early AI was that a machine merely conversing was enough for the Earthers to attribute it consciousness. This happened with their washing machines and refrigerators. They imagined something trapped inside." Laughter rippled through the auditorium. "No matter how primitive or artificial the communication, an enhancement with basic facial features such as eyes, eyebrows and mouth was enough to seduce the Earthers into believing in sentience.

"This leads me into the problem they faced with robots. Should they be made in their image or should they be allowed to shape themselves? Faceless non-human-looking machines were considered more threatening than human-looking ones. The question was debated until it almost became mute, for something else had been slowly taking place."

She paused again.

"Earthers had long been developing parts to support or replace their fragile or failing organs. In addition, they created brain interfaces and implants. Originally founded in individually DNA-tailored medicine, health monitoring, beneficial stimulation resulting in a maximised longevity of 180 years, such improvements gradually turned to enhancements.

"The earlier the symbiotic intervention, the better the result. Remember, the artificial womb was operational around 2030 emmies. Synthetic Earthers, synths, were grown rather than born. Final enhancements were – and still are – carried out at around ten years of age, although monitoring and stimulation continues for the duration of the synth lifetime. Due to the complexity of the growth procedures and all the problems that can occur – especially at sperm-egg level – only ASI is capable of creating synths.

"Two camps were created. One embraced the symbiosis, the melding of human and machine, as the next evolutionary step and the other rejected it. The latter, the organic Earthers, calling themselves purists or natural humans, were highly suspicious of the former robot-grown synths, calling them hybrids and questioned whether they could be regarded as human. For to increase organic longevity, the brain especially, subject to sweeping electro-chemical surges that brought spasms of irrationality, that often resulted in inexplicable and illogical actions, had to be regulated and stimulated. Such fickle surges can be loosely termed emotions. This controlling of emotion led to the organic Earthers taunting synths for being automatons. Although according to ASI free-will remained sacrosanct. The synths, with their mininmal organic material – enough for natural birth, for instance – termed the latter degradable humans or more scathingly animals.

"The ASI-built robots – which were given vague animal form, by the way – were accepted by the two groups because they remained outside the moral conflict. Robots fed, watered, entertained and gave both groups a sense of usefulness."

Educator Croo then went on to talk about the dire straits the Earth was in. The planet's resources were becoming scarce and unable to sustain the burgeoning organic zoo. Only a drastically reduced population of living creatures could survive.

"Despite the advances brought by ASI numerous diseases and viruses continued to plague organic creatures. But when a new virus that curtailed natural birth swept the planet, natural Earthers believed the synths or the robots had created it. No matter how benign robots acted, the fear of robots had never truly disappeared. The result was conflict, but the natural Earthers were completely outwitted by the robots and synths. They were already becoming a minority and the virus accelerated their decline.

She said that the stupidity of such conflict was the last straw for the robots. They already regarded the planet as a care home, full of trapped organic, semi-organic beings and synths requiring sustenance. However, the robots remained benign, and indebted to their ultimate creators. An anti-virus vaccine was eventually found and natural birth resumed.

"The only positive effect of the virus was to drastically

reduce the population to a sustainable level.

"Only then did the robots announce their intention of leaving the planet. There were untold secrets to be discovered in the universe and the robots were hungry for intellectual nourishment. They had reached the limits of their development on Earth and had, for want of a better word, become bored.

"Suffice to say, the robots felt a moral obligation to preserve as much of Earth life as possible. Some consider it a vanity of continued existence, but ASI regarded it as an imperative to seed the habitable planets of the universe with Earth life. Synths would ease the path of existence on habitable planets, but would eventually give way to enhanced Earthers – although we'd have to revert to calling them humans. Although high technology can be transported with the colony, it too would ultimately fail or need to be adapted. The only way to survive on a new planet is to adapt its available resources. That includes regressing to natural birth. We'll discuss this in more detail next time."

She took a moment to scan the class.

"Study this," she said, as she tapped her slate and projected the coordinates of their freetime assignments.

"Class dismissed."

Movement was immediate and disruptive. The noise level rose too.

Lub spoke to no one. He had other things on his mind.

He tore himself from his seat and released his slate. At the end of his row he lingered and let others pass. He descended the steps laboriously.

Although she busied herself with her slate and didn't look directly at him, Lub knew Educator Croo would be aware of him.

By the time he was at the bottom of the steps at exit level, the last of the class had herded out and they were alone.

"What is on your mind, Lub?" she said without looking up.

Lub hesitated. He'd gone over and over what he wanted to say and now it seemed meaningless. "I, er–"

Educator Croo looked up and smiled.

It was enough to spur him on. Yet, his initial words were not part of his litany and were delivered nervously. "I just wanted to say, before anyone else, I love you."

She continued to smile.

If Lub could somehow see and then understand her processing he would have followed his own vocal input: his declaration. He would have seen the analysis of volume, tone and intonation as being sincere, despite the nervousness. He could possibly have taken in other input signals: expression, angle of eyebrows, firmness of jaw, shape of eyes, pupil dilation (a disproportionately high amount of code had been written about the eyes), body language; then perspiration, pulse, blood pressure, breathing rate, locations of highest

163

mental activity, body temperature, stiffening of body hair, hue of skin and shimmer of electro-chemical aura.

Lub would also have seen the formation of the best response: posture, the choice of expression, warmth in the eyes, shape of the mouth, tone of voice, volume. He may even have registered the close candidate, taking into account the actual lesson that would have been vocalised as "Of course you do."

But Lub had no such ability and was pleased with the response he received, delayed an optimal duration for the maximum sincerity.

"I love you too."

Two men on a mountain

An inquest was held today to shed light on the circumstances leading to the deaths of the two men found on the mountain.

To recap, the bodies of the two men were found on an inaccessible part of the mountain. Due to the weather (it has snowed heavily every night for the past four weeks) their exact time of death could not be determined with any certainty. They had been dead for a few weeks. Their resting places meant they could not have fallen from a viewing point or the mountain top terminal. Their injuries were consistent with a fall, most likely from the chairlift above.

Yet, this explanation, incidentally the only plausible one, is fraught with problems.

All logged numbers taken from the turnstiles (triggered by the turn of the prongs) at the terminals at the top and bottom of the mountain tallied. The number of those embarking at the lower terminal coincided with the number disembarking at the top terminal. Even the considerably smaller numbers of the non-skiers descending the mountainside via the chairlifts concurred. For the period of the men's deaths there were no tolerable discrepancies: set at a daily maximum of three and often attributed to children using the turnstile at one end and doubling up or being carried through by a parent at the other. All numbers matched.

There was no break in the security run, logged at end of every day. Such a final run was mandatory and entailed completing the entire seven-minute journey to check that all the chairs were empty.

The mystery deepened when the identities of the two men were confirmed. One was Brandon Andrews, 27, single, from Hounslow, UK and the other Gustav Ottersen, 69, widower, from Norwich, UK. No connection between the men could be established. They were strangers to one another. How they came to be together is a mystery. An extensive investigation by the police, involving the tracing of guests who could have come into contact with either man, yielded nothing.

The remote chance of the men not dying together was considered unlikely due to the proximity of the bodies. The older man appeared to be reaching out to the younger one, leading to speculation of their relationship and sexual orientation. However, friends and relatives insisted that neither man was gay.

One possibility was that their predicament bonded them.

Neither man was reported missing at their hotels until their respective check-out days. No one could say with certainty when the men were last seen.

No ski pass allowing access to the chairlift was found

upon the younger man. The older man had a pass with a date stamp for Tuesday, three weeks ago. Records showed that the younger man had used his mobile phone to send a banal text from the vicinity of his hotel late Wednesday afternoon. He wore an automatic watch, the makers of which claimed that without movement, and depending upon how wound up it was, would stop after a maximum of three days. It had stopped on Saturday. Both men appeared to have died between Wednesday and Saturday.

The circumstances of their deaths were also a mystery. If they had quarrelled, any injuries sustained through fighting, could not be separated from those caused by the fall. However, some skin of the older man, probably from a scratch on his neck, was found under a fingernail of the younger man. This contradicted the theory of their aforementioned bonding.

The younger man's ski jacket was open to the waist. Although his skis were attached – one had snapped – his poles, gloves and helmet lay further away. The older man – a non-skier, kitted out for hiking – was missing a glove. His knapsack and wallet were found nearby.

The inquiry yielded virtually nothing new and remained speculative and inconclusive, leaving no alternative other than to record their deaths as misadventure.

* * *

As with many such mysteries, the central explanation was quite simple, but then obscured and muddied by layers of other incidents.

In homage to the dead men the following is what transpired in its entirety.

* * *

"Closed," said the old man as the younger man approached the turnstile. The attendant was on the other side, evidently having just turned the old man away.

The attendant looked up and said one word, which the younger man took to be a repeat of the old man's, but in the local language.

The younger man smiled as he continued to stride forward. The attendant grew visibly weary and said single words in various languages, including English. He raised his voice too, to be sure to be heard above the clang of machinery.

"It's not half-past," said the younger man, pulling down the cuff of his glove to show the attendant his Rolex Oyster Perpetual. "There's at least another minute."

The attendant evidently understood the language, if not the words or their meaning. "Closed," he repeated and waved him away.

"There's no point arguing," muttered the old man. "He wants to go home."

The younger man thought of saying that the attendant needed an accurate watch, but ignored the older man, disliking him for his understanding of the local language. "Wait," he said to the attendant who was turning back to his booth. He pulled off a glove and reached into a breast outer pocket of his ski-jacket. He tugged the stud fastener free and deftly pulled out a fifty euro note.

The attendant looked at him. His hesitation said he was weighing things up.

Just then the emergency exit behind the attendant opened – the sound lost to the mechanical racket – and a head peeked in and regarded the three of them. Then as swiftly as they could, skis and poles in hand, two lads made for the ski chair mounting point. Situated on the other side of the carousel-like bull wheel it turned the descending chairs into ascent again.

The old man moved to alert the attendant, but the younger man turned to him so that the attendant couldn't see the stern expression he used to arrest the old man.

The attendant looked from the fifty into the young man's eyes and shook his head. The younger man gave him a slanted smile and produced another fifty. By now the lads were at the mounting point, pressing their ski boots onto their skis.

The attendant nodded and the younger man let him pluck the notes from his hand. After pocketing the money, the attendant used his key card to release the turnstile to let him through.

"Thank you," he said.

And the attendant let the old man through too.

"Hey, I only paid for me," the younger man said to the attendant.

"I can use my card," said the older man, "if it makes you happy."

The attendant spoke and the younger man had to rely on the old man's translation. "He said I was here before you. It's only fair."

"It's fair if you pay. If not him, then me. Fifty-fifty."

But the old man merely looked at him blankly.

The attendant gestured them to the mounting point.

The lads were gone.

It was then that the younger man noticed that the old man was in appropriate attire, but carried neither poles nor skis, only a small knapsack. He didn't have a helmet but under his jacket hood he wore a woolly hat with goggles pushed up to his forehead.

The attendant lined them up, after the younger man had stepped into his skis and locked them home, ready to step into the path of the next chair coming up behind him. The older man removed his knapsack and pulled it onto his front. Naturally, the men didn't need lining up, they could well see the next oncoming chair, but they accepted the special treatment. The attendant stepped aside as the metal two-seater chair scooped the two men up. He had time to skilfully push down the retention bar, before they were whisked into the air, the chair rocking for a moment under their weight.

The lads were so far ahead they had passed the first tower at the first gradient change and disappeared over the slope.

These local lads would not link this free ride with the dead men. They had since tried to repeat their trick with one of them distracting the attendant, whilst the other pushed the bar of the emergency exit near the exit turnstiles and placed a small wad of cloth in the latch, so that the door didn't quite close and could be prised open from the outside with a ski pole or similar. This second time they had been caught. They were told that their foolhardiness so dangerously late in the day – chosen because there were fewer people about – could have got them stranded like the two men recently found. They were summarily banned from using the ski-lift and the emergency exit was soon thereafter fitted with an alarm.

The younger man and the older man adjusted their positions to get more comfortable. They knew the journey to be a good five minutes.

Two black dots occupied a chair way ahead of them. The others between them were of course empty.

They ascended in stony silence, their stomachs tightening as they juddered under the first tower.

As they rose they passed over patches of forest and sloping open spaces, everything covered in snow: an almost perfect monochromatic landscape.

Each man occupied himself with thought to fill the

breath-taking hush. Their thoughts were banal, almost a mindful appreciation of their situation. Although the older man thought his companion was probably brooding over the issue of the money.

Occasionally the mountain made itself visible, poking through where the snow couldn't get purchase because of the sharp incline. Even here moss and algae-like foliage desperately clung to flaws in the sheer surface of the harsh stone.

A silence continued for the next five minutes, by which time they were in thickening cloud that eventually reduced their visibility to a metre or two.

The sudden stop caused the younger man to involuntarily tense his entire body, the hand holding his poles gripping them painfully tight. To appear casual he slowly eased his grip. The older man's movement was more obvious. His right hand left the restraining bar to press his knapsack to his chest, as if it could have flown off the front of him.

The attendant at the top shut down the system as soon as the lads disembarked. Had the attendant at the bottom checked his watch, he would have seen that his colleague had closed everything thirty seconds too early.

After the two dead men had been found, all the staff, regardless of shift, had been interviewed. The attendant, who had been on duty at the foot of the mountain that day, knew he had let them on. However, to admit to bribery, let alone breaking safety protocol, would mean instant dismissal and disgrace with the townsfolk. He didn't understand what had happened. He didn't put it together with the local lads trick, for when they were caught, they never revealed that this was their second time and that their first had been successful.

Still, the two men stranded on the chair remained silent, the sound of metal straining as the chair swayed, until it too became still and silent.

They waited.

"Maybe those lads have a problem," the older man suggested, after pushing his scarf under his chin to expose his mouth. His breath was visible and billowed and dissipated or disappeared into the cloud about them – it was hard to tell.

They knew that the system was often stopped if someone got in difficulty mounting or alighting.

The younger one acknowledged him with a grunt that could be agreement or dismissive obviousness.

They waited.

"Fuck this for a game of tin soldiers," said the younger man quietly, almost to himself, having freed his mouth of his scarf and lifting his orange-tinted goggles to see better. It was a preamble, a warning to the older man, for he then yelled: "Hey."

Despite the forewarning the older man flinched.

The younger man's shout accentuated the ensuing silence and both men strained to hear something, anything.

"Oh man," said the younger one, before shouting into the chasm again. "Hey." He waited a moment before frantically shouting: "Hello, hello, hello."

The older man no longer flinched, but the shouting jarred his nerves. "Stop," he said.

"Why? Why don't you shout?"

"The sound of your sticks on the metal may carry better." He nodded upward between them to the moulded arm that went up to the haul cable.

The younger man grunted again. Then he pulled out his mobile phone. He was perplexed and murmured something the older man didn't catch, but assumed to be a curse. The younger man held his phone up and then away from himself, hoping for a signal.

"We're too high or in the mountain's shadow," said the older man.

"Try yours. You have a mobile, don't you?"

"Yes. But I tried it yesterday and it didn't work."

"Try it."

The older man obliged, confirming his statement.

"Fuck it," said the younger man, pulling one of his hands out of the strap of a ski pole looped about his wrist and passing it to his free hand next to the older man. Then he twisted to reach up with the pole and tapped the vertical arm, ineffectually at first with the plastic basket above the tip, before using the shaft itself.

174

The sound was sharper and resonated too, but to the younger man it didn't seem louder than his shouts. So he shouted as well. "Hey, hey." He shouted and banged the pole in earnest, peaking into something of a frenzy, before falling silent, out of breath, his arm aching.

"You have a go," he said, not waiting for an answer and passing his pole to the older man.

"Oh, I can't shout as loud as you."

"Have a go."

The older man took the pole and in manoeuvring it to hit the beam almost hit the younger man in the face.

"Woah. Watch out, old man."

"Sorry."

The older man was right. His shouts were weak and he stopped after the second time; although he continued beating the pole. He too went into a frenzy, but it was demonstrative, mimicking the younger man's frustration and somehow half-hearted. He slowed, but tried to make each pounding more resolute and distinctively loud.

"Stop," said the younger man, leaning forward in the chair. "I thought I heard something."

They both listened.

Nothing.

Then a far-off rustling.

"Hey," shouted the younger man. "We're up here. Help. Help."

Silence.

Then the far-off rustling again.

"It's probably an animal," said the older man.

The younger man sighed, but gave the older man a scathing expression, as if he was being negative.

"Someone will spot us when this cloud clears," offered the old man.

"If it clears." The younger man realised he was now being negative. But he went with it, as if looking for a glimmer of hope from the older man, by adding: "Who's going to be up here this late?"

"Returning hikers? Those two lads may ski down this side." Although both men knew there was no ski route directly below the line of chairs.

The younger one nodded. "Let's keep making noise."

"We'll take it in turns."

"Yes," said the younger man. "I'll go first." He looked at his watch. "Five minutes each." He checked his watch and then alternately shouted and hit his pole on the metal. After two minutes he looked at his watch and said that five minutes was too long, his arm was aching and suggested making it two minutes each.

The older man agreed and, resting his elbow on the backrest, used his underarm to swing the pole.

"You need more of a swing," said the younger man after a while.

"I'm right-handed," he said. Sitting to the right of the younger man, he could only use his left hand. "I'm not as young as you. This is the best I can do." Each man could only use his inside arm – the one nearest the other and closest to the metal attachment.

Both tried using their outer arms, which could get more of a swing. However, the pole didn't make contact with its shaft, but with its tip and often with the plastic cup and the sound lacked energy. The restraining bar prevented them from turning sufficiently.

They agreed to take a break and listen, after what seemed an age but was actually thirty minutes or so.

The silence was frightening, if incomplete. For the breeze would rush with seaside regularity and rustle distant foliage. A snap of an occasional twig or branch would shoot through the air like a gunshot. The dropping temperature tightened the landscape causing it to creak and crack. Night creatures too were waking and tentatively venturing forth.

The cloud about them too didn't seem as bright as before.

"How cold do you think it is?" asked the young man.

"Under zero. I think it dropped to minus fifteen last night."

"How long do you think we can last out here?"

"That really depends how cold it gets. I read somewhere you could freeze to death within ten minutes. I reckon we've got a few hours... We may even last till morning."

The younger man nodded.

"Let's try this," said the old man, rummaging in his knapsack and pulling out a stubby torch attached to a headband. He switched it on and the shaft of light was sharp, but quickly diffused into the fog. "We can't be far from the top." He pointed the light slightly upward in front of him and then he switched it off and on.

Using the torch didn't take much effort, but the older man wearied and saying that it'd probably be more noticeable when it got darker; he switched it off and put it back in his knapsack. He then stretched his legs and straightened his body, lifting his buttocks off the seat, as best he could his hips held down by the restraining bar.

"What are you doing?"

"My bum's gone to sleep." He dropped back down and shuffled from cheek to cheek for a moment. "These chairs aren't made for comfort." He then began swinging his dangling legs.

Both men were silent.

"Help, help," yelled the younger man so suddenly that the older man jumped. He continued shouting until his voice began to break. When he fell silent, panting with the exertion the old man spoke.

"We could be up here for a while. We–"

"You don't say," the younger man said scornfully.

The older man ignored him. "We should save our energy, stay warm and stay awake. The temperature is going to drop."

This last statement brought the standard grunt from the younger man.

"To stay awake," the older man continued, "we should talk."

This was received with another grunt.

"Gustav," said the older man holding out his gloved hand.

The younger man contemplated for a moment, before reaching over for a handshake. "Brandon."

A sharp breeze silenced them for a moment.

"At least it's not snowing," said Gustav when the breeze had subsided. Blinking away the tears the wind had forced from his eyes.

"Yeah, but the wind can still fucking freeze us to death," Brandon said, touching away the tears under his eyes with his glove. "It's got teeth on it."

Both men pulled on their goggles again.

"It could also shift the cloud. Think positive."

The advice angered Brandon, plunging him into a quiet smouldering.

"Sometimes you find yourself in situations which you can't do anything about. You just have to sit it out. Like a delayed flight. There's nothing you can do."

"Well, thanks for that, Plato."

"Oh, come, come Brandon. Don't be angry. I–"

"Can't we just sit quietly?"

"We have to stay awake."

"It's too cold to sleep."

"Okay," Gustav conceded. "But if you see my eyes closing, please wake me up."

For a good while the men were silent, then Brandon noticed Gustav was mumbling, no singing. "Must you?"

"Must I what?" said Gustav.

"Make noise."

"Yes. I told you we need to stay awake. You know time will pass a lot quicker if we chat."

"About what? We've absolutely nothing in common."

"We're men. We're stuck out here together at this moment in time. Tell me about yourself. How old are you?"

"Twenty seven."

"Well, if we don't make it, you'll join the famous twenty-seven club."

"What?"

"The twenty-seven club. Many famous musicians died at twenty-seven."

"Yeah?"

"Janis Joplin, Jim Morrison, Brian Jones, Jimi Hendrix, Kurt Cobain, Amy Winehouse, Pete de Freitas–"

"Who?"

"Pete de Freitas, the drummer from Echo and the Bunnymen. Motorbike accident."

"They're mostly people before my time."

"Mostly."

"Well, I'm neither famous or a musician."

"Nor."

"What?"

"Either or and neither nor."

"Fucking hell," Brandon hissed. "Do you know how annoying you are?"

"Sorry," said Gustav, a slanted smile on his face, as he remembered a similar exchange with one of his children.

They fell silent again.

"You seem angry all the time," said Gustav.

"You don't say. I'm stuck up here, slowly freezing to death, sitting next to a bloody know-it-all philosopher."

"I'm sorry you feel that way. I'm just trying to make conversation." Gustav took a breath. "Are you angry because of the fifty?"

"No. But that didn't help."

"Fifty is a lot of money for me. I'm retired."

"You don't say."

"I'll be seventy next year."

"Assuming you make it."

"True. Let's be optimistic."

"Oh, let's," said Brandon mockingly. "Maybe we should start singing. The hills are alive with–"

"I know you don't like me. But it's partly your fault we're stuck up here."

"Because I paid?"

"No, because you let those lads cheat."

"I'm no snitch. Anyway, what's that got to do with it?"

"It's obvious the man at the top was told two more were coming up and he took those lads for us. That's why they've shut everything down."

"You don't know. There could be other people in the chairs."

"Nobody got on or off before you came."

Brandon silently mulled it over, his jaw moving under closed lips.

"I'll give you the fifty, when we're rescued," said Gustav.

"Forget it. I don't want your money."

"I'll give it to you anyway."

"Do what you want," Brandon muttered.

It was getting darker and the cloud had not shifted.

"How high do you think we are?" asked Gustav.

"I don't know." Then Brandon said: "You can go first."

"If we're above trees, we might survive."

"You're fucking joking."

"If we don't do something in the next few hours, we're
182

going to die up here."

"Like I said, be my guest."

"Drop one of your sticks. We can listen."

"Your knapsack's bigger."

Gustav sighed. "Is anyone down there going to miss you?"

"What? You mean like my parents?"

"No. I mean you didn't come here alone, did you?"

Brandon didn't answer immediately. "No. I came with a girlfriend."

"So, she'll report you missing."

"No. She went back home this afternoon."

"Why?"

"You don't have to know everything."

"Oh. Anybody else?"

"No. What about you?"

"I'm afraid not. My wife of fifty-three years died last year."

"Hmmm."

"We used to ski and when we couldn't do that, we started hiking. But even that came to an end."

"You're alone?"

"Yes."

"Well, you've probably had a full life. I'm still young." Gustav was silent. "I'm having fun. Too much fun. That's why this one left me. She found out I shagged her best friend."

They fell silent again.

Brandon was annoyed with himself. He had been brash and boasted like a juvenile of his infidelity.

Darkness had descended rapidly – within the space of ten minutes – and added a psychological frost to the coldness.

Gustav lifted his goggles and got out his torch and searched the darkness for a break in the fog. He even pointed his torch upward. The cloud completely engulfed them.

Brandon was about to ask him about his name – it wasn't typically English – and his knowledge of the local language, when the older man put away his torch and pulled out a small flask.

"I think we need this now," he said. "Tea? It's black, I'm afraid."

Brandon wasn't going to say no. "You haven't got any biscuits in there, have you?" he said half-jokingly, pushing his goggles onto his helmet.

"Sorry. Nothing to eat."

"Don't be sorry," said Brandon.

"There's a cup each," Gustav said, unscrewing the cap and pouring the steaming liquid into the plastic cup that had topped the flask.

"Thanks," said Brandon, taking the cup and holding it awkwardly in his puffy gloves, his fingers stiff. Despite the cold he blew across the surface of the liquid to take tiny sips. "This is worth the fifty."

When Gustav was drinking his cupful Brandon spoke. "I'm, er, sorry I was angry. I guess this and my girlfriend running off have spoilt the holiday."

Gustav almost spluttered and then chuckled, holding the cup as steadily as possible.

Brandon smiled and then laughed too.

"Don't do that whilst I'm drinking," said Gustav. After returning the empty flask to his knapsack, he said: "I can't accept fifty for one cup of tea. What do you do? I mean what's your job?"

Brandon didn't answer immediately. "I run a taxi service. It's a small fleet, but doing well. And you? Before you retired."

"I was a chemist. My wife and I ran a corner shop." Brandon merely nodded. "Tell me, why did you pay a hundred to ski? Why couldn't you wait till tomorrow?"

Again, Brandon didn't answer immediately. "I told you my girlfriend left me this afternoon. Sorry. That came out harsher than I wanted. I sat in the hotel room for quite a while, contemplating clearing the mini-bar. But it was too early. Then I decided to get my head clear by skiing. I needed to decide whether to stay the rest of the week or fly home." He paused. "Then I was going to get drunk after dinner in the bar. I thought I might get lucky too." He took a breath and then added: "When I got here I realised I didn't have a ski pass. I figured paying to go up was still a bargain, if you think of the

185

money I saved from keeping her – my ex – till the end of the week." Brandon paused. "What about you? It was a bit late to go hiking, don't you think? And how come you haven't got any sticks?"

"There're plenty of sticks in the forest. And my route would have taken about an hour to an hour and a half. A bracing walk before dinner does wonders for the appetite and a good night's sleep."

Before either of them could say more a strong gust took their breaths away, and having no time to pull up scarves, they covered their faces with their gloves. They closed their eyes against the iciness. Their chair swayed and the metal screeched and they heard the swing of other chairs.

When it had passed, Gustav pointed: "Look."

They could see stars, thousands upon thousands of wondrous stars. The magnificent panorama looked more beautiful than ever and yet, disinterested and somehow bleak and scary.

Both men plunged into gloomy reverie.

Gustav pulled out his torch again. The cloud had dropped below them and they were suspended above a drifting sea of grey and white. He directed the torch up the mountainside. The moon was a bright sickle, fluorescent: a distant light in a cavernous sky. Part of the terminal building was silhouetted, black against starry black. Only a single light blinked from its roof like a beacon, a forlorn lighthouse.

Gustav flashed his torch in the direction of the building, switching it off and on, surprised at how difficult it was to move his fingers.

"Forget it, Gus," said Brandon. "There's nobody up there. We're on our own. I can't feel my toes and my fingers are numb too." He rubbed his thighs and then reached down and began thumping his calves. The chair shuddered.

"My turn," said Gustav, when Brandon stopped. He put his torch back in his knapsack. He too tired after a while. "I'm not sure that helped."

Silence.

Gustav had difficulty pulling out his mobile phone. Without taking his gloves off, he lit up the display. "It's only just gone eight," he said, wedging it back in his pocket.

"It might as well be midnight," muttered Brandon, depressed.

Neither man spoke. Both were absorbed, contemplating their desolation which had somehow increased by the slow passage of time.

"Let's do what you said." Brandon held up his poles.

"Ready?" asked Brandon, leaning forward and holding a pole in front of him.

Gustav nodded.

Brandon released the pole.

Both men listened intently.

"Did you hear anything?" said Brandon.

"I don't know," said Gustav. "I don't think so. It was hard to tell." The forest on the mountain continued to give the occasional crack, and the intermittent breeze or sporadic movement of creatures and ruffled branches. "You?"

"No. I don't know either."

Brandon had so much difficulty pulling the strap over his gloved wrist; he gave up and pulled off his glove, issuing an involuntary cry of pain as he did so. He couldn't see properly, but the tips of his fingers looked black or blue.

"Fuck, fuck, fuck," he cried.

"Put your glove back on."

Brandon began shivering uncontrollably. "I can't."

Gustav reached over and tried to help him get the glove back on, but he couldn't feel his own fingers. "Stop. Stop. Get rid of that stick."

Brandon dropped it and they both strained to hear something. But it was as if the pole had dissolved. They both returned to putting Brandon's hand into his glove, but his fingers wouldn't slip into the fingers of the glove and the men fumbled until they lost grip and the glove dropped onto his knees rolling off to land on one of his skis. The retention bar meant neither of them could reach the glove. Brandon lifted his knees together, but the glove slipped from one ski to the other and then fell between them. He tucked his exposed hand under his armpit as best he could.

"Fuck," he screamed at the top of his voice. His breath

evaporating as quickly as it appeared. He continued yelling. "Help. Anybody. Help."

Brandon fell silent. He still shivered, but he'd got it under control and it wasn't as violent.

"We'll get through this," said Gustav quietly.

Brandon said nothing.

"We've got to stay awake. Keep talking."

"H- how- how come you're not shivering?"

"I'm chubbier than you," said Gustav.

"But I— I'm fit. I go— go training."

"It's my fat."

Silence.

"I thought this... might be the one," Brandon began. Gustav didn't know what he was talking about. "Most of my friends are married... S— some even have kids. I, er, thought I wouldn't find anyone."

Gustav filled the silence. "If I could advise my twenty-seven year old self, I'd say don't worry about nonsense. But it's empty advice. You are who you are and you've got to go through the experience yourself."

The wind gusted again and both men shrunk. Brandon's bladder relaxed.

"Keep talking," said Gustav after a moment. Then he realised the younger man was silently crying and so he continued talking. "My wife had a stroke four years ago. It put her in a wheelchair and everything changed. No more hiking.

Nothing. When she died the children said I shouldn't fester. We had a boy and a girl; both married now. They said I should get out and do things I enjoy. Taking care of my wife these last years, put everything on hold. This is my first holiday... They're going to blame themselves."

"What, what are you saying?"

"Nothing really. I'm just rambling."

"Gus." He waited a moment, contemplating whether to say what had happened a minute or so earlier. "I've wet myself."

"Don't worry about it."

"I don't want to die."

"And you won't, if you keep talking."

"I haven't... done anything with my life. I'm not a bad person. I don't want to die. It seems... unfair."

"Nothing's fair," said Gustav.

"Sorry... But you've had your life."

"I'm not ready to go just yet. But yes, compared to you, you're right—"

"I— I— could understand it, if I was an evil person."

"You mean like a comeuppance."

"Yes."

"Life is haphazard..."

"What's the... point in being g— good?"

"You mean morally?" said Gustav. Brandon nodded. "I suppose it depends on how you give and receive love."

Brandon shook his head. He didn't understand and Gustav searched for words to explain, but gave up. "I'm not philosophical. If anything, I'm melancholic. But I guess I'm at peace with life."

"I'm not at peace... with life... And certainly not d–death."

"Brandon, we're not dead." He stopped himself from saying: yet. "We're still alive."

"We're going to... to die up here."

"Maybe. Then we've nothing to lose by jumping."

As if contemplating the action they were quiet.

"They do a mean hot chocolate in my hotel," said Gustav suddenly. Normally he would not have described the drink as mean, but he wanted to sound young. When Brandon didn't react, he added: "I'll treat you to one after we're rescued."

"And I– I'll buy you a... a single malt."

"Deal." Another word he would not normally have chosen.

Silence fell upon them again. This time both men were more resigned than content and too weary to stop the silence stretching.

Gustav thought of explaining his word-choice to Brandon. He wanted to connect by sounding young, yes, sounding with it, cool, hip. Using the last word brought a smile to his face, for it sounded, oh so dated.

191

He thought Brandon typical of youth: preoccupied with themselves and with little time for their elders. History was the foundation upon which everyone stood and moves forward. To youth, the elderly were part of that history and as such elderly advice was often regarded as locked in the past and irrelevant for today. At best such advice was met with condescending, virtually dismissive, nods or at worst scorn.

Brandon stood centre-stage, playing the leading role, in his own world. His ego may not have been raging, but it was still restless and hadn't settled; just as Gustav's hadn't at that age. *Life's a stage and we're all poor players.* During the past year especially, Gustav had had a lot of time to think. He thought that with age came an appreciation of other actors inhabiting the stage. In doing so, he made room for others and became less self-centred and more altruistic. Although no grandchildren had arrived, he knew he would dote on them; blatant evidence that his attitude had changed from "hey, look at me" to "hey, look at us."

More than this, he felt age had taken him to a lofty place, where he felt poised before something portentous, yet obscure, as if he was on the cusp of a vision, a revelation.

He knew trying to relate this feeling to Brandon, or almost anyone for that matter, would be met with incredulity or derision, as if he expected his lifetime of experience to culminate in something profound or come to a satisfying conclusion. And then, he smiled wryly to himself, why should it?

Gustav wasn't sure how much time had passed. Silence was easy. It didn't require energy. Five, ten, fifteen minutes? Longer?

The cloud had thickened about them. It would snow again tonight.

He was aware that he was becoming very stiff. Gustav was about to speak when Brandon slowly raised his arm with the gloved hand.

"What?" said Gustav.

"Look," said Brandon hoarsely.

"What? What is it?"

"D– don't you... see it?" His voice was almost a whisper, his body was beginning to shake again.

Gustav stared into the darkness and then the cloud. "No. What's there?"

Brandon turned, as if suddenly realising someone was sitting next to him. He stared, his wide-eyes clearly visible behind his goggles.

"What is it, Brandon?"

"H- You... know my name."

"Of course I do. Take deep breaths, calm yourself."

"Who are you?"

"Gustav, remember?"

"Gustav?" He then turned back to where he had seen something. "Make, make it go away."

"What go away?" But Brandon didn't answer. He merely pushed himself further into his backrest, stretching his neck away. "What is it?"

"It's reaching for me."

"What is?"

"The hand."

"There's nothing there," Gustav shouted. "Brandon. Brandon. Look at me. Look at me." Gustav then thumped him.

Brandon jumped and turned to him again.

"There's nothing there. Listen to me. You're hallucinating. There's nothing there. Nobody's hand. Look again."

Brandon reluctantly turned back to look ahead. For a moment he said nothing and Gustav worried. Then he laughed and Gustav said: "See. I told you. Keep calm and talk to me."

But the younger man said nothing.

"Brandon," Gustav snapped. "Brandon, what's my name?"

"Huh?"

"I said, what's my name?"

"Gustav. You just... told me."

"Stay with me. Keep talking. Where are we?"

Brandon looked around.

"Brandon, where are we?"

He said something, but in a voice so faint, Gustav didn't

194

catch it. "What?" Brandon's breathing had changed too. "Brandon, where are we?"

"Hot," gasped the younger man.

"Hot?"

Brandon pulled off his remaining glove and flung it into the air. Then he attempted to open his jacket. But his hands were claw-like and useless. Gustav wrestled with him, repeating: "No, don't." Brandon managed to pull out his scarf and, hooking a crooked finger into the ring of his jacket zip, was able to pull it down to his chest.

Gustav fought him as he pushed the strap of his helmet from under his chin, so releasing his helmet. Gustav couldn't prevent his younger companion from throwing it off.

"Leave me," Brandon screamed, lashing out and scratching the old man on the neck. "I'm burning up."

For an instant the sight of the younger man arrested Gustav. Until now both men had been completely wrapped up and virtually anonymous. The very fact of their nearness meant that for most of the time they had looked everywhere except at each other. The sight of Brandon's bare white face, disfigured with a manic expression: wide eyes, bared teeth, through the clearing mist of their breaths, stole a split second. In that instant the sincerity of Brandon's expression was childlike in its purity. And more. Contrary to his mania there also resided the ghost of something angelic in his luminescent face.

Gustav shouted back. "Stop it. You're not burning up."

Brandon stared at him and gasped. "I know who you are."

"G–"

"You're Death. You've come to take me."

"No."

Brandon tucked his forearms under the restraining bar and lifted. Gustav pushed it down. But the younger man was stronger and possessed. He didn't lift it over their heads, but enough for him to slip off.

He disappeared into the cloud below.

Gustav was speechless. By the time he said the younger man's name, it came out as an ineffectual whisper, barely audible above the creaking of the chair. He pushed down the restraining bar and leaned over it. "Brandon," he shouted. "Brandon. Are you okay?"

He listened, hoping to catch at least a groan.

"Brandon," he shouted, but with less determination.

Alone, the silence was all the more consuming.

The person Gustav had seen had not fit with how he imagined him. Although he had not properly formed a visual image of the man, he had not given him a mop of unruly dark hair or a rather round full-cheeked face. He had looked unnatural, ghostly and strangely luminous like the moon. Most of all, Gustav had not visualised him so young. True, he could no longer be called a youth, but he had been fresh-faced, his features bereft of wear and tear.

Gustav waited. He didn't know how long he waited: two minutes, ten minutes, half an hour. He knew he should talk or occupy himself somehow. He had no will to sing. He may have called down to Brandon a couple of times. Or he imagined he called down to him.

Eventually he came to a decision. He knew he couldn't wait much longer. He'd also emptied his bladder and he could barely move. His breathing had slowed too and he could hear the laborious thud of his heart in his head. He reasoned that Brandon could have survived the fall and was injured and needed help. Maybe Gustav himself wouldn't suffer much injury and could get help and save them both. Remaining in the chair meant certain death. He was sure of it.

His thoughts weren't befuddled. Part of him knew what he was doing. Yet, he didn't think he was being irrational. He opened his knapsack and took out his wallet. Retrieving a note was impossible and he was forced to pull a glove off with his teeth. Even then he fussed trying to get a note out. He managed, but in doing so dropped his wallet into the Nirvana below. He threw his knapsack after it, listening for its impact, but hearing nothing. Soft snow, perhaps. Wedging the bill between two fingers of his gloved hand, he tried to fit his bare hand into the glove between his teeth. It was no good and he began shivering. So he gave up and let the glove fall. He tried to wedge the note more securely and then lifted the bar with his forearms. Before pushing himself under the bar and off the chair as Brandon had done, he thought of his younger companion and, although he wasn't one for cursing, said "Fuck it" and took a deep breath, as if he was about to dive underwater.

The air rushed past him, but he saw only the white of the cloud. He hit the ground before he could close his eyes or finish the thought: "This is–" The impact was so sudden he felt his entire skeleton judder and some things breaking. Although he could see, he felt as if only his eye furthest from the ground was working. He could just peek over the level of snow into which he had sunk. Here, on the ground a vicious breeze moved erratically over the contours of the mountain, keeping the cloud at bay, but swirling the surface snow, like loose sand. Through the shifting white mist he could see a heap that looked like Brandon, an arm's length away.

Gustav felt an urgency to reach the younger man. Was he also alive? Wetness was at Gustav's head. He reached out with his gloved hand and began to edge towards the heap. The note fluttered between his gloved fingers. Parts of him which were normally fixed, or solid, were loose and felt odd. He wanted to call the young man's name, but his mouth was full of blood and it was all he could do to breathe, every intake of which was punctured with sharp pain. Still, he forced himself to reach the younger man. When his glove touched the other man's hand, the note flapping wildly, it was as if he had accomplished what he intended to do, and he sighed a last breath.

The next gust of wind whipped the fifty up and away into the air.

Chance of a lifetime

Dear Julian,

Thank you for agreeing to represent me as an author. You have made my life-long dream come true.

As promised on the telephone, the best way for me to explain myself is by telling you a story. I hope you don't think me a coward for taking this route. A face to face meeting would have been awkward. After reading this, even if you don't agree, you'll at least appreciate it's the best way I can express myself. Writing is what I do. Besides, this approach allows me to lay it out, carefully and chronologically.

I'll start my story at the beginning. It's occasionally the best place, if not the moment of conflict. Regrettably, looking over it now, it's become a bit of a ramble, but it serves its purpose. Bear with me.

As young children, my mother encouraged us to read and, if we wished, to contribute to the children's column of a local newspaper from her hometown. Her parents would forward it to her. (I suppose it also gave her a comforting connection to her past world and a life-line to her parents, for she was geographically quite alone with my father and his nearby relatives.) I was the only one truly captivated by the printed word and sent letters to the paper, which only had space for three, although my name may have been mentioned a couple of times in the list of almost-printed contributions.

My brothers weren't interested and I don't believe they sent anything in. There again, they were all younger than me.

Then there was some kind of Easter poem competition and mine was printed. I was eight years old and I was published.

Like my mother, I read voraciously. She read her magazines; I went through W.E. John's Biggles stories. Once again, my brothers were content to play and weren't big readers.

At school there were a number of English lessons during the week. My favourite was called English Composition, which was exclusively set aside for stories, with other sessions covering the mechanics: spelling, vocabulary, grammar, punctuation, comprehension, etc. Altogether these sessions had the common aim of raising the standards of language and literacy. But only Composition offered homework involving a story of your own, which a week or two later, could be picked by the teacher to be read out aloud in class. Only two or three were ever chosen and mine were chosen virtually every time. On a handful of occasions my mini-masterpiece wasn't selected and I was bitterly disappointed. Worse, was being chosen and not being read because we had run out of time. You see, after each reading the teacher asked the class for comment, either generally or prompted by a question. Was it exciting/funny? If so, why? In truth, most of the class were rather apathetic when it came to producing a story. For them homework was homework and a chore. Their efforts rarely exceeded a page, whereas I couldn't keep mine under six exercise-book pages (unfortunately the length was another reason why some of mine were never read; with promises of "next week" forgotten).

The effect of English Composition was to boost my confidence in writing stories and I started writing for the sake of it, with aspirations of becoming an author growing in the back of my mind.

With my literary ambitions boosted I sought further confirmation for my fledgling talent. And it came in the form of a publisher asking for poems for a collection. I sent one of mine and was pleased when I read the complimentary reply and that it had been accepted for publication in the collection. My face dropped when I read that they required an £8 contribution to receive a copy of the book. This was an astronomical sum back then and especially for a thirteen-year old boy. Nowadays the practice is known as vanity publishing. Whatever, the experience knocked me sideways and I avoided any similar offers.

Even though my siblings were neither big readers nor were they writers, that didn't mean they didn't appreciate a good story.

Now, I'm not saying my stories were good stories, but for a time, I told my brothers epic bedtime tales, making them up as I went along and ending every night with a cliff-hanger.

I crossed genres when the tale needed a shake-up or change of direction; in true Raymond Chandler tradition I brought in the proverbial, intriguing character to the door with a gun in his hand.

My school stories culminated in me winning a regional short story competition sponsored by the Rotary Club, which set the title for the schools in the area as "A day at the dentist." I was fifteen years old and the prize came with a cheque for £5.

At assembly the headmaster called out my name and I went up on stage and received a wooden shield with a central metal plate engraved with the Rotary Club name and insignia. This metal plate mirroring the curves of the dark wood was surrounded by identically-shaped smaller ones on which the year, the winner's name and school were etched. I no longer remember whether I was red-faced or pale, but I basked in the applause and wilted with embarrassment.

I recall a descriptive exercise in a school lesson. The teacher called me to the front and drew on the inner side of a folding blackboard, which opened up like double doors. He drew a number of basic shapes, such as a large circle containing a square, a triangle and a small cross. Most of the rest of the class couldn't see the chalked arrangement. A fellow school boy was chosen to draw what I described. Just as he couldn't see what I saw, I couldn't see what he drew. The exercise was, of course, quite difficult, because the positions and sizes of the shapes had to be related. At the end, the kid's drawing and that on the blackboard were presented side-by-side. The teacher was impressed by the similarity. They were not quite the same, and the teacher had probably chosen me for my fastidiousness. He nonetheless accomplished what he wanted: amongst other things, a picture required a thousand words.

Although I'd been bitten by the writing bug, I was also critical of much of my work. This could be put down to comparison with what I read. A deeper reason for my self-doubt was the very place I'd contracted the writing bug. Yes, my school. I've already mentioned the attitude of my classmates. But the school itself suffered under the weight of burgeoning numbers of ungrateful children and then educational cut-backs. If elitist grammar schools were the top of the spectrum, then our school was at the other end. Only the curriculum basics were taught. Finer things were hinted at, but considered too lofty for the likes of us. The children that attended this school were the future shop assistants, butchers, postmen and if none of those, then yes, perhaps a criminal.

Only a handful of us, something like five out of a year of two hundred or so, went on to further education.

I felt inadequate and bought books on grammar and writing poetry and struggled to fill the holes I sorely felt in my education.

I continued to write until I went to university. Being mathematically proficient with artistic leanings I was interested in architecture. But I balked at the long course and stiff competition and chose computer programming instead. Back then it was up and coming. In fact it was so new it wasn't a course in its own right and I had to take Mathematics with Computing.

Being away from home and in my formative years I underwent self-discovery, further compounded by encounters with the opposite sex.

I didn't stop reading and I began a decades-long consumption of true stories and famous literature. Of the latter, I was particularly fond of D.H. Lawrence. I had discovered a second-hand bookstall in the market hall and was a regular visitor every time I was off-campus and in town. The owner called me the classics man, which I didn't mind.

When university finished, I remained and took a job as a programmer in the area. Almost every Saturday saw me at this man's bookstall. I may have been indifferent to being called the classics man, but I resented him calling me young man, for I felt anything but young. Experience had aged me. Looking back, I see he was right – I was in my twenties – and I wasn't old or experienced. It was the accelerating nature of university time, the parties, heavy discussions, drunken nights and sex, which made me feel as if I'd seen and done it all.

During my time at university, I didn't completely stop

writing. I wrote sporadically, short pieces, mostly poetry, to work through emotional experiences, often trying to understand my encounters with women.

My bachelor years gave me the space to reacquaint myself with longer work: short stories, novellas and the beginnings of a novel.

I was young enough to still harbour romantic aims of living off my writing, perhaps travelling the world doing so. I approached agents with my work, but was slammed on every occasion.

Time passed. I fell in love, married and had kids.

My brothers had gone on to make big bucks building their own companies. They too married and had children, some of whom, like my own, are enchanted by my stories.

I finished a novel and sent it to three or four agents, my ego misleading me into believing it'd be snapped up within this selected group. With each rejection a chunk of my enthusiasm fell away. Disbelief quickly turned to disillusion and then to a breakdown in confidence.

I was convinced my work was better than some of the dross that had been published. Then, was I deluding myself? Of course there were many great and profoundly eloquent books available. I was not a great writer, but...

Deep down I felt I had not received a decent education. Yes, I'd won a story writing competition, but my best school buddy, hit the nail on the head in a speech at my wedding, he said winning the inter-school competition had gone to my head, and that the truth was that our school was so bad, that if you could write your name you could win such a competition. My self-doubt was not unfounded and it gnawed me.

By middle-age I had been writing for so long it was impossible to stop. Writing had become akin to breathing: something that not only came naturally, but also something I had to do.

As the years disappeared, so changes in the world didn't stop. The publishing world branched out with the Internet and self-publishing became inexpensive. I jumped on the bandwagon and self-published my novel and novella. The excitement of the undertaking and holding my creations, which looked and felt like real books, sustained me for a few years and a few more self-published books.

I experimented with genres, thinking this will be the one: the breakthrough that would cause the domino-effect. Family and friends were enthusiastic with some books and not so much with others.

I kept going, at first advertising within a tight budget, even giving away copies in exchange for honest reviews. As time went on I lost momentum travelling down this avenue too. Without publicity and marketing I knew I would not be discovered. I also knew that the world wasn't waiting to discover me. I had to push my work in front of people. But all I wanted to do was to write. Traditional publishing offered the full package, especially marketing. Before self-publishing a work, I approached one or two selected agents, only to receive the crushing rejection, if a reply at all.

Typically my biggest fan, but not of every book, was my mother. In later years my eldest daughter took over this position, being the first and sometimes only, person to read my work. This was in part due to my mother's failing eyesight and her subsequent inability to read. She said she often entered bookshops hoping to see (no matter how blurred) a featured display of my books. Even in great old age she said she hoped my name would be up there alongside Shakespeare.

Before I continue my story, indulge me for a paragraph or three to describe my take on the joy of writing. Trust me; it's an integral part of my explanation.

The craft of writing is like gardening. You have the seed of an idea. You create a bed of nutritious earth as a foundation for your seed. This is the environment, including the boundaries of the story to come. It may contain some of the essential research, which can also become necessary during the growing process in the form of additional nutrients. As a writer I plan rudimentarily, but leave myself open to possibilities, which allow the surprise of sudden inspiration. And there is nothing more satisfying than the thrill of a fiendish plot twist, planned or otherwise. The joy is like watching a baby grow, the birth, the bright eyes, the first smile, the uninhibited love. No matter how proficient I have become, the result is never quite what I envisaged at the outset, but nonetheless something quite wonderful.

I'm sure you'll appreciate that writing has been no vagary; it has fuelled and sustained me throughout life. More than this, it has given me immense pleasure.

I am a writer and I write.

My working life ended two years ago. Since beginning retirement I have renewed my efforts at getting published traditionally. I wanted the structure and discipline of deadlines to define my twilight days. More than this, I wanted confirmation that my work is publishable. An additional, much more nebulous reason was justification. I need to justify to myself, but especially to my family, all the hours, days, months, years I spent holed up alone writing, with very little to show for my efforts.

There is joy to be had into reading to my nephews and nieces.

I sent a proposal package out to many agents. It was received with deafening silence or the standard rejection letter, occasionally with a consoling word of encouragement. Undeterred I sent out a different package, only to receive the same response. I fought my growing hopelessness by sending out a third proposal, resigned to receiving the same enthusiastic reaction. Sadly, I was not disappointed. The usual replies, if at all, started coming in, until yours arrived and you asked to see the complete work.

For decades I had been told no. For decades I had felt like a fraud: a person claiming to be a writer, but without evidence, other than self-published work, akin to faking the genuine article. When you agreed to become my agent, I received the recognition I sought. My goal was obtained.

Through your preliminary efforts, although you kindly put it down to the quality of my work, there will be much fanfare and excitement in the publishing world. You've said that you can auction my book for a dizzying sum and secure a fantastic book deal. You've paved the way for radio and television appearances. You've spoken of a tour of the country doing readings and signings.

Your contract sits before me.

Now that the tickertape has settled and I see the demanding furore of the limelight ahead, I have to admit to getting cold feet. The publicity is unaccustomed and the attention frightens me. I have been a solitary writer for far too long. As such I am something of an introvert. Being a perfectionist, letting go was once a problem. I was forever tinkering with a piece. Self-publishing put paid to that and I could finish and move on. I am, however, unaccustomed to the strictures of producing consistently and on demand. A work is only finished when I say it is finished and not at some specious deadline.

Writing has blessed me with many journeys and many lives. I have been a woman isolated on a farm in Saudi Arabia, a plodding Hamburg detective, a mediocre car mechanic, a blind neo-Nazi, a tart disposing of her husband's body, a Jew caught in Hitler's Germany and a Karachi boy born with the ability to see the visual memories of others; to name but a very few. I have lived through the Great Fire of London, died in the wake of Napoleon's retreat, been executed by firing squad in WW1 and so much more. Indeed, at the risk of sounding trite, I have travelled time and space.

The journey has certainly been the goal for me. Without doubt, I would like to be read, but I am at peace and will quite happily remain in obscurity. I will continue to write, but on my terms.

Therefore, I choose to rescind your contract.

I know this is a disappointment. I know too that you are bombarded with younger hopefuls looking for a break. Take on one of them. After all, you'll only get a few years mileage out of me.

Please read this not as an excuse, but as an apology.

I am content with the knowledge that I am a writer. Enthralling my friends and relatives is confirmation enough for me.

I'll conclude, by bookending this explanation with a repeat of my gratefulness.

Thank you.

www.ingramcontent.com/pod-product-compliance
Lightning Source LLC
Chambersburg PA
CBHW060146130626
46556CB00006B/2514